Postcards
from South Africa

BY THE SAME AUTHOR

The Middle Children (Second Story Press, Toronto, 1994)

Eyes of the Sky (Kwela Books, Cape Town, 1996)

The Slave Book (Kwela Books, Cape Town, 1998)

Sachs Street (Kwela Books, Cape Town, 2001)

Confessions of a Gambler (Kwela Books, Cape Town, 2003)

Postcards
from South Africa

by Rayda Jacobs

DOUBLE
STOREY
a juta company

First published 2004 in southern Africa by Double Storey Books,
a division of Juta & Co. Ltd, Mercury Crescent, Wetton 7780,
Cape Town

ISBN 1-919930-61-2

Edited by Helen Laurenson
Text design by Catherine Crookes
Page layout by Claudine Willatt-Bate
Cover design by Toby Newsome
Printed by CTP Printers, Parow, Cape Town

Contents

The beginning years

The new South Africa

Acknowledgements

The first twelve stories in this book first appeared in *The Middle Children*, published in Toronto in 1994, and are of especial significance because they are the 'fledgeling stories' – stories written while I was living in Canada, longing for home. This was the first time I wrote about a girl called Sabah. After my return to South Africa in 1995, I wrote more stories and, again, Sabah appeared in one or two. It was inevitable that the two groups of stories should come together in one book. There is no one definitive South African story, and the collection is made up of 'Cape Flats' stories, 'township' stories, 'Muslim' stories, and others. The stories span 50 years, and serve as a background for Sabah.

Some of them have been published in anthologies and collections:

'Lady, That's the Rules' in *At the Rendezvous of Victory*, Kwela Books, Cape Town, 1999

'The Guilt' in *New Writing*, Picador, London, 2001

'You are the Daughter' in *Opbrud*, AKS/Hjulet, Denmark, 2000 and *Post-Traumatic*, Botsotso Publishing, Cape Town, 2003

'Sabah' in *Wespennest*, Germany, 2003

Dedicated to the memory of my mother, Amina Jacobs,
who passed away as this book was going to print,
on 4 February 2004. 'Don't mention it'
is specially dedicated to her.

The beginning years

Madula

The hole was in the middle of the yard, between the stables and the chicken run. Sabah knew the diggers: crippled Cupido, who lived in Mr Hennie's shed on the other side of the soccer field, and his pal Marco. Swart Piet was too old and arthritic to climb in and dig, although he was in charge, every so often swearing at something on his right shoulder, laughing for no reason at all.

Dullah, in black rubber boots, khaki hat and shorts, a cigarette behind his ear, stood with Swart Piet, looking down at the diggers as the shovels kicked into the pit and deposited huge mounds of earth at their feet.

She walked up gingerly. 'Granpa Doels?'

Dullah Solomon looked up. He was enormously fond of this child. She was the first grandchild. He'd never been a father. Sabah was the daughter of his wife's son. Everything he loved about children was in this child.

'What're you doing out this early? And without your gown and shoes?'

'I wanted to see them dig the hole.'

'It's winter, you'll catch cold. Now go inside before Little Granny sees you.'

'Granpa?'

'Yes?'

'Can Christian people dig the hole for the Qorban?'

'It doesn't matter who digs the hole; it's the deed that counts. God accepts everyone's good work.'

She was silent for a moment, squinching her toes in the wet grass. It looked like no good deed to her. She had tossed all night in bed thinking about how Madula would die. Would the cow snort and kick her heels in the dust, refusing to come to the hole? Would she feel the cold steel of the knife? Would she die right away and not feel anything? A faint drizzle touched her cheek. She looked up. The sky looked weepy, and she wished it would rain and drown everything out, forcing her grandfather to cancel the Qorban.

'I think He's a selfish God.'

Dullah turned, surprised, but she was already walking back to the house.

Swart Piet cackled as he relit a half-smoked cigarette, shouting down to Marco not to throw sand on his feet.

'That cookie's a Solomon, all right.'

Dullah smiled. 'Okay, Marco, that's deep enough.'

Cupido and Marco handed up their shovels, and climbed out.

Swart Piet fitted the wide plank along the edge of the hole, knocking each end into the earth with his cracked boot.

'Good job, Cupido, thank you,' Dullah said, handing them each five shillings. 'Don't forget to come by this afternoon for your meat.'

They nodded their thanks. Cupido took off his hat, scrunching it unconsciously in his hands. 'As Baas vir my die kop kan hou, asseblief? If it's not too forward to ask?'

Dullah was a novelty to his Christian neighbours. He wasn't like any other Muslims they knew. Owning racehorses and cattle, he went to the track and threw jazz parties on New Year's Eve. Dullah would turn a blind eye to workers throwing dice, but drew the line at liquor on his premises. He gave generously to anyone who asked: it didn't matter whether you were in rags or in silk. People knocked on his door for food, odd jobs and loans, and he often created projects for them, upsetting his wife, who still reminded him of the crooked brick braai wall a gardener thought he could build.

'Old Madula's head? Of course. I'll save it for you. Not many takers for brains and eyes, although my wife likes the tongue. It makes a good roast. Fried brains and onions can taste just like omelette.'

Cupido smacked the hat on his head, showing a nicotine smile. 'Dankie, baas.'

'Don't call me "baas", Cupido.'

'Okay, baas.'

Dullah's wife, Janey, was in the kitchen, slapping her hands into dough when he went inside. He could tell by the ridge between her eyes that panic was setting in. It was just after seven in the morning and, by noon, the house would be crammed full of people. Janey's daughters were due to help with the breyani and curry, but he knew from Janey's mutterings that she would still fiddle and fuss, even though the meat had been prepared, marinating in green coriander and yoghurt overnight, and the puddings and trifles were all done.

'I need some help in here,' she said.

'Why are you making roeties also?' he asked. "It's too much work. There's rice.'

'Roetie tastes better with lamb curry. Can you put out the ginger beer on the stoep?'

'Where's Sabah?' he asked.

'Inside. She came in with wet feet mumbling about something. Her mother's coming to pick her up this afternoon. We don't want any performances. And make sure she's wearing warm clothes. Don't let her catch cold on her last day here and we get the blame.'

'What's for breakfast?'

She shot him a look. 'There's porridge in the pot. Don't still bother with eggs. There'll be no place in this kitchen in half an hour.'

Her long hair was twisted into a bun at the back of her head, and he came up, pulling out two of the pins.

'Stop it.'

He pulled out the last one, watching the coil jump down her back, and quickly escaped into the front bedroom, where Sabah was rummaging through her suitcase. 'And what's my little Masquerade wearing today?'

She held out her plum corduroy pants.

'That? There'll be girls here in sequins and pearls. Your cousins, too. Don't you want to be the prettiest? What about that nice green velvet dress with the lace your mommy made?' And he slipped in what had to be said: 'You know she's coming today.'

'I don't want to go home, Granpa.'

'It's school tomorrow, Sabah. You promised her you wouldn't carry on like the last time.'

'I can live here with you and Little Granny. You can drive me to school.'

'Your mommy will miss you. She misses you already when you come for the holidays.'

'She won't miss me, she has Oemie. I don't like it there. With Auntie Kareema and my other cousins next door.'

'You've been here for three weeks.'

'And my daddy? Will he miss me when I'm gone?'

'Of course.'

'I don't think he likes little girls.'

'Why do you say that?'

'He never asks if I want to come with him in the car, and he never does anything with me. Mommy says I come here for him, but I don't think so. You remember I told you about my friend, Shirley? Her father takes her to ballet lessons every Saturday. And when I go there to play, he takes us to the park. Even though the park's right at the back of the house. I want a daddy like other people, Granpa. My friends don't believe I have a daddy. They say I made him up.'

'Where do they think you came from then? The wind?'

She searched around for her socks, a serious look on her face. 'Can you have children, Granpa, without a husband?'

'Of course you can,' he laughed. 'You can have anything you want if you put your mind to it.'

'Anything?'

'Anything. If it sits in your heart long enough, you get it. But be careful what you wish for.'

'Why?'

'Because not everything you wish for is good for you. Now, what were you saying about God outside?'

'I said He's a selfish God. Why does He want us to kill Madula for Him?'

'He doesn't want Madula. You know the story of the Sacrifice. It's to remember what Abraham did.'

'But it was cruel of God to expect Abraham to sacrifice his son. Would you do it, Granpa, if you had a vision from God? And God asked you to sacrifice me?'

Dullah laughed. 'Maybe that's why I don't have children. God knows I'm weak. And Abraham didn't go through with it, remember? At the last minute the lamb came, and Ishmail was spared.'

'But what if the lamb didn't come, Granpa, and Abraham really sacrificed Ishmail? What then?'

He studied the serious little face with the freckles on the little nose twitching in consternation. 'But it didn't happen that way, did it? It was a test for Abraham and he passed it. He didn't question God's will. And when he told Ishmail what he had to do, Ishmail agreed. Abraham listened to God. And the son listened to his father. There should be a story about little girls listening to their grand-fathers.'

'Don't be funny, Granpa.'

He laughed, scooping her up onto his lap, and putting her down again. 'Go and brush your teeth, I'll put out your clothes. You can wear your corduroy pants until the people come, then change into your dress. And be careful you don't get it dirty and wet.'

'I still don't see why Madula has to be killed. Can't we just buy meat from the butcher? She isn't a regular cow, Granpa. She loves Piet and gives us milk every day.'

'Exactly. There are uses for animals. In the desert, camels carry loads and give milk, and their hair can also be woven into cloth. Cows and goats and sheep are useful to us. When they're sacrificed, we show that we're willing to give up some of our own benefits for others.'

'But why must you do it, Granpa?'

'Because God gave me a lot. And,' he smiled, 'a man with my many sins must do some things right.'

She frowned, wrinkling her nose. 'Being a Muslim is hard, Granpa. God wants too many things. Look at how many times He wants us to pray. Shirley only prays on Sundays. And then she gets to wear a new dress.'

Sabah watched with two cousins from Masquerade's stall as her grandfather, Imam Hosein, with his white robe and gold-threaded headgear, and her uncles and nephews and friends came from the kitchen into the yard.

Swart Piet removed Madula's bell – the bell that had so irritated Mr Pietersen down the street – lightly tying a rope around her neck, the free end attached to the loquat tree at the side of the house. It had all been unnecessary. Madula was resting under the tree. There was about her a silence and calmness, as if she knew.

Swart Piet talked to her in that rumbling way he had, rubbing her flank, and wrapped a cloth loosely around the head, covering her eyes. Tugging gently on the rope, Madula followed him to the pit.

There was a murmur in the crowd when they saw the blind-folded cow.

Testing the sturdiness of the plank with his foot, Swart Piet tapped Madula on the flank, and the cow buckled her forelegs and went down, her head inches away from the pit.

'Let's go stand near the hole,' Gadidja said. 'I want to see.'

'Yes. It smells in here,' her sister, Sadia, agreed. 'Look at my shoes.'

'I'm staying,' Sabah said, her patent leathers rimmed with manure.

'Heretjie, look at Alavia's hair. Do you think she puts stuff on it to make it so red?'

'No. They all have that carrot hair – like they were dipped in rooibos tea.'

The others laughed, and someone shouted for them to keep quiet.

'Isn't your father helping Granpa Doels to slaughter the cow?' Gadidja asked.

Sabah pouted. 'I don't know.'

Behind them Masquerade dropped a load. They wrinkled their noses in disgust.

'Our clothes are gonna stink.'

'Your grandpa isn't his father,' Sadia said.

'Whose father?'

'My mother says Granpa Doels isn't your father's real father.'

'Your mother's a liar! Granpa Doels is!'

'She's not a liar!'

'She doesn't know anything, she works in a factory!'

'But she didn't marry a half-naartjie, did she? Can't you see? Your father's white, your grandfather's black!'

'My grandfather's not black!'

'Bismilla Hiragman Nira'him,' the Imam started.

'And he has a girlfriend!' the sister threw in.

Three men manoeuvred the cow on its side. Dullah took a rag from his pocket and soaked it with chloroform.

'My friend ...' the Imam started. 'We can't do it like this.'

'It's a small mercy to the animal, Imam.' And he applied the wet cloth to the cow's nostrils and mouth. The men behind him sucked in their breath. This was way out of line. It was a mockery and might even contaminate the meat.

'A girlfriend?' Sabah turned to look at her.

'Yes. Your father has a girlfriend! That's why your mother left! She found out!'

Sabah punched her in the face. 'It's not true!'

'Fiekie play too much with his dicky, everyone says!'

Sabah punched her again.

Sadia's glasses fell off and she fell flat on her bum in the hot shit.

'Call your mother now, four eyes!' Sabah kicked her as Gadidja opened her mouth to scream.

The Imam started the prayer, Swart Piet rubbed a few drops of water over the cow's face. There was the flick of the knife, then a sudden spurt as the blood drummed into the hole below. The onlookers watched in silence as the cow gave a last heave of breath, then came slowly to rest on the plank.

Gadidja screamed. Sabah was on Sadia's chest hammering with her fists when Little Granny's wooden spoon whacked into her behind.

'What's going on here? Sabah!'

Sabah turned. Next to her grandmother, Granpa Doels stood in stained pants, slowly nodding his head.

Miss Pretorius

Mrs Verkeer was in the kitchen peeling potatoes for supper, listening to the radio, when her serial was interrupted by the news.

This is a special bulletin. Prime Minister Verwoerd was stabbed to death today during a session in the House of Assembly ...

The potato dropped into the sink, and she looked at the radio as if it could confirm that she'd heard right. Hendrik Verwoerd? Whaaahh Ghottala ... and she ran out of the house, not sure what to do, who to share the news with. Would old Mr Lewenberg next door have heard? Maybe he was sitting on the stoep and didn't know. She got to the gate, wiping her wet hands on her apron, and spotted Mrs Prins across the road bending down in her garden. She wouldn't speak to that Nosey Parker. She quickly turned back inside. Would Evvy know? Of course she would. They played radios in offices now. She would call her daughter at work. Being in the heart of town, Evvy would know more. She was proud of her daughter, of her good job as a typist for architects. Still unmarried at 29. Mrs Verkeer had great faith that soon the Lord would send the right man for Evelyn. She dialled the number, wondering what her tenant, Miss Pretorius, would feel, knowing what she knew of the young history teacher. The cheek of the girl. The audacity. Did she have no shame?

The following day, still shaken by the news, the schoolteacher could tell from the vibration in the classroom that little time would be devoted to lessons that afternoon. Cape Town rocked with the news. The assassination had provoked international cries of dismay.

'Good morning, Miss Pretorius.'

'Good morning, class. Please sit down.'

Her top student put up his hand.

'We'd like your opinion on the assassination, miss.'

'I don't deal in opinions, Ivan. The fact is, we lost a prime minister last night.'

'YESS!!'

Another student had up his hand. 'Clive?'

'Do you think that whoever gets to be elected now will be more liberal?'

'We're in the world spotlight, who knows?'

'I mean, he got it good in the neck. They should start watching their backs.'

The whistling and desk banging was deafening.

'Class!'

'We've been centre stage before, what's new about that? We don't need a Winds-of-Change speech,' Ivan continued; 'we need some serious arse-kicking *bringing* change!'

The noise flared up again, and the teacher banged on her table with a book.

'You're out of order, all of you.' But there was amusement in her eyes. 'I'm leaving this class for five minutes. When I return I want you turned to page 109.'

She walked briskly to the staff toilets, taking a swallow of water from one of the taps. The overhead mirror showed a young woman with a blush complexion – a euphemism for not quite dark – broad nostrils, pretty eyes, kinky hair straightened into a stiff bouf-

fant. Miss Pretorius would not be mistaken for white. Miss
Pretorius didn't want to be white. But Miss Pretorius had a secret
that made her sweat at nights. What would her parents say? Her
students, if they knew? The face in the mirror shouted, Hypocrite.

Her parents were out on the Cape Flats, but she lived in the
renovated servants' quarters of Margaret Verkeer, a Seventh Day
Adventist, and her frumpy daughter, Evelyn. Sometimes the old
girl would come and have tea with her in the small kitchen and
she'd help her fill in forms Mrs Verkeer didn't want Evelyn to know
about and, often, a plate of pineapple fritters waited for her on the
kitchen sill at the back. Yesterday a note with a single request was
under the door.

Shortly after midnight, in bed, charged with the words of the
Lord, Mrs Verkeer didn't have to hear the hinge on the gate to know
the lover had arrived. She was familiar with the engine sounds of the
taxi and, in the moonlit room, his shadow danced on the wall as he
catfooted past her window down the cement path to the back. At
dawn the same taxi whisked him out of the neighbourhood. How
could Miss Pretorius do this to them? What if anyone were to look
out their window and see? Especially that Mrs Prins? It would be all
over the neighbourhood: a white man coming out of Margaret
Verkeer's house! Tomorrow she would have a word with her tenant.

But the next day the man from the Municipality came – they'd
heard there were servants' quarters not shown on the building
plans – and Mrs Verkeer was kept busy mollifying him with pan-
cakes and tea, forgetting all about her talk with Miss Pretorius. The
teacher didn't respond to her landlady's request, so it was
Wednesday before Mrs Verkeer, seeing the glow of the kitchen light
on the guava tree in the yard, quickly took herself to the back.

'Miss Pretorius,' – she caught the teacher in the middle of supper – 'I've got to talk to you about something that's been on my

mind. In a way it's none of my business, but then it also is. What I mean is — '

'Is it about Michael?'

'Michael?'

'My fiancé.'

'He's your fiancé?'

'We're getting married in December. I was going to come and talk to Mrs Verkeer and give notice at the end of the month.'

The air went out of Mrs Verkeer like a slow puncture. 'Married? You and him?'

'And as Mrs Verkeer knows, we can't live here in South Africa until they scrap the Act. So we're moving to Bechuanaland in the New Year. I hope Mrs Verkeer understands.'

Mrs Verkeer was properly stunned. 'Well, that's a horse with a different colour, isn't it? Marriage. I see. I mean, it's only because of the neighbours, you understand. The law. I mean, I don't mind, but if word gets out, you know how spiteful people can be.'

'Michael and I don't want trouble. He likes this country, coming from such a damp place as England, but we have no choice now but to leave, as if being in love is a crime.'

Mrs Verkeer tried hard for a smile. To her, it *was* a crime. That flatnosed Miss Pretorius with her kaffir hair and Bushman lips breaking God's commandments could land a man, a white one nogal – good-looking, well-dressed – and her church-going daughter with green eyes and straight hair couldn't find anyone. Where was the justice in that? What did this platkop have besides lifting up her skirt for a man?

'I'm sorry if I've caused Mrs Verkeer any worry, but I can't say enough how relieved I am that it's finally out.'

'And your family? They don't know about him?'

'Not yet. My father has a bad heart, he won't take it well.'

Back in her own kitchen Mrs Verkeer found her daughter clearing away the supper dishes. She filled Evelyn in on what was happening with the tenant in the yard.

'You mean that girl brought someone here all the time, right under our noses, a white man, while we were asleep? How disgusting!'

'Can you imagine if Mrs Prins should look out her window and see?'

'The whole world will know. Did Ma get a look at him? What he looks like?'

'He's nothing much,' Mrs Verkeer lied.

'She's trouble, Ma, let her go. We won't have difficulty finding a good tenant.'

'She's leaving at the end of the year. And she promised he would only come weekends now.'

'But how can you let it go on? What if people find out? You're allowing sin on the premises.'

'I know. But can you believe it? He wants to marry her?'

'I don't know what he sees in her. She must be good under the blankets. It's the quiet ones. You never can trust them. Get rid of her, Ma, let her go.'

Walking home from church that Saturday, Mrs Verkeer came around the corner of her street and too late saw Mrs Prins catapult herself from her gate. 'I hear you gotta midnight visitor these days.'

'Me?'

'Lewenberg says he hears the gate at night.'

Mrs Verkeer had thought the old man asleep by nine.

'A white man comes to your teacher in the back, did you know? With a taxi. In the middle of the night.'

Mrs Verkeer took a handkerchief from her clutch bag and

dabbed at her face. 'My own little Miss Pretorius, are you sure? She's such a decent girl.'

'You mean you don't know what goes on in your yard?'

'I'm asleep by ten, Mrs Prins. I don't hear anything.'

'You heard what happened to Hettie's son, didn't you? A Portuguese living with that loafer son of hers in the back and the Security Police came in the middle of the night. At three o' clock when even God's taking a nap. They banged down the door and charged in like animals and woke the whole neighbourhood up, dragging them out by their necks and keeping them ninety days under the Act, troo's Gawd.'

Sweat pearls formed in the groove above Mrs Verkeer's upper lip.

'People are spiteful,' Mrs Prins continued. 'You don't know who will give the game away.'

Mrs Verkeer crossed the road and found the teacher sunning herself in the yard. 'I just ran into Mrs Prins, the biggest busybody in Athlone. She tells me everyone knows what's going on.'

'But how? Michael only comes on Saturday nights.'

'She says old Lewenberg next door hears the gate, but I think it's her.' Mrs Verkeer pulled at the weeds between the geraniums. 'I know I said you could stay till the end of the year and I haven't changed my mind, but people are sitting at their windows with binoculars now. I must ask you not to let him come to the house anymore. Is that a terrible thing to ask?'

'No problem, Mrs Verkeer. We only have a few weeks to go anyway.'

'Thank you. I'm sorry, but you know how it is.'

'I understand, Mrs Verkeer.'

The taxi stopped coming and the weeks passed. When Mrs Verkeer ran into Mrs Prins again, the focus was on another neighbour whose teenage daughter's pregnancy had just come to light. Mrs Verkeer was glad that Mrs Prins's malice was channelled elsewhere.

On New Year's Eve the cars lined up outside the house as people came to say goodbye to the teacher. Listening to the music and laughter, Mrs Verkeer felt strangely out of sorts. Something nagged at her. It was the same uneasiness as the time she'd dozed off on that hot afternoon when Willie was ill, had a dream that he was floating face down in the Liesbeek, and found him dead of a heart attack in the bath the next day.

At eleven she decided not to wait up for Evelyn and went to bed. The stress of the last few months had drained her. She thought her daughter could've gone to the back and wished the teacher well. It cost nothing to be nice, and it took courage to put your life in a suitcase and leave. South Africa, for all its *krake*, was still home – even if the blacks took charge she wouldn't leave. And what had Miss Pretorius really done? She could write a clever letter, and had indeed saved her from the Municipality. Perhaps it was that Miss Pretorius was more decent than some of those starched virgins hallelujahing it up in church that weighed so heavily on her mind.

Somewhere around four, when the night was still and you could hear the Devil breathe, Mrs Verkeer came out of a fitful sleep. Was it the gate? Something in the next room? She watched the trees sway like dinosaurs on the bedroom wall and tried to pinpoint where the sound had come from. But nothing moved. A cough on the other side of the wall reassured her that Evelyn was home. Maybe it was her daughter coming in or going to the bathroom that had woken her up. Still, the uneasiness squeezed at her chest and she recognised that feeling of doom.

The curtains stirred in the breeze, her heart picked up a beat. In the distance she felt them approach. Silent as serpents, then the screeching brakes, voices barking through the front door.

Masquerade

The rain dripped from the roof of the stoep, sparkling like crystal studs on the leaves of the hanging vine. For a moment Sabah fastened onto the cellophane drops in the winter sky, promising hope, tomorrow, when the darkness would lift and everything would be gone: the bier with its red satin dome, the silent, bleak-eyed women grating camphor in the living room, the sickly sweet smell of day-old corpse mingled with dried rose leaves and condensed-milk tea, the lorry waiting to take the cottonwool-packed body to the mosque. Her other grandfather.

Where was her mother?

She saw the birds gliding in a V over the house. Something squeezed in her chest, she couldn't breathe. She was cold with two jerseys on and had to pee but was afraid to go to the toilet. He had fallen in there. First the cup from his hand into the terrazzo tub, then him onto the tiled floor. Dead as they carried him down the hall. The house felt as if something lived in the walls: clammy, threatening, waiting for her in the passage to reach its dank hand into her neck.

'Mommy?'

No one else was on the stoep. Should she peer in? The curtain wasn't drawn all the way. No, she would be sick, like the time she'd been forced by Miss van Graan to go to a Christian boy's funeral. The marble face with the spittle on the blue lips. And that smell. The body had been in the coffin for two days and, in the heat, the rot had clung to her uniform. She could still see the old lady with the rolled-up newspaper swatting the flies.

But she was curious. Four men had gone in. What were they doing in there? What was a heart attack? Looking sideways without turning her head, she backed closer to the window, collecting her strength. Turning slowly, she pushed her forehead into the pane. It took a few moments for her eyes to adjust to the body on the katel, a metal table with a drain, a bath underneath catching the water trickling down. A white sheet covered the body. The men had their hands wrapped in white cloths, and were positioned at the head, feet and arms, washing the body under the sheet. Then one of them lifted a foot and she saw the leg move. It frightened her. It was a dead body in the room. Her mother's father. He wasn't going to be at the supper table with them anymore. When he was in the hole the angels would come, and the sand walls would squeeze him if he'd sinned.

'Hey, what are you doing looking in there?'

She turned at her aunt's voice and ran from the stoep into the rain. The owls would come tonight, she thought. They had come for three nights, and then her grandfather had died. They should be satisfied now, and go away.

Someone loaded her onto the lorry with twelve other kids. Girls were not allowed in cemeteries. Maybe she looked like a boy with the new haircut her mother had given her. 'Don't still make frills 'n' drills with that hair,' her grandmother had said. 'Soon she must wear a scarf. And she's six already, why do you let her wear pants?'

The earth was red, gravelly and wet. Three men were in the hole: two positioning the body facing east, the other fitting the planks. Wedged tight in his cave, his roof at right angles over his head to wait for Judgment Day. For the angels to come and ask what good he had done and testify against him if he lied. Would the linen come loose and the sand drop on his face? How long would it take for the skin to crawl with that other life? Would they curl through his eyes like caterpillars or come slithering through his mouth? And what if his soul *hadn't* left through his collarbone like the Book said, and he was shouting with unmoving lips that he was still alive? And felt the sand coming down?

'Make sure you're wearing clean panties, you're going with Moena and Juleiga to the calipha's house,' Auntie Kareema said.

'Why?' Sabah asked her aunt. She'd been at her aunt's three days now while her parents sorted out their troubles, and wished it was already suppertime, when her mother would pick her up. All her mother's sisters, especially Auntie Kareema, disliked her father. Auntie Shamila wasn't bad, she sometimes joked with her father, and the two of them would laugh, but Auntie Kareema and Auntie Jaweier didn't like her father and didn't like her because she looked like him. 'White Fiekie,' they called him – Fiekie for Shafik. Still, it was better here than at Auntie Zanap's next door, where all the boys called her names.

'You can't send her without Aisa's permission,' Shamila said.

'Those women are only there today. You know they don't do it openly anymore.'

'They shouldn't be doing it at all. And it's not your business to send Sabah. Aisa's her mother.'

'They don't really do anything, they just look.'

'You know they don't just look.'

'We went, didn't we, when we were kids, and it didn't do us any harm?'

'You went, not me. Anyway, it's wrong and has nothing to do with God. It's something men came up with to keep women under control. Because they can't control themselves, they want us tamed like yard cats. The imams do nothing about it.'

Kareema wiped at the perspiration on her face with her scarf. 'It's wrong to speak like that. Do you want to be cursed?'

'Why must I go, Auntie?' Sabah asked again.

'You ask too many questions. Run along.'

Sabah felt hurt at the harsh way she'd been dismissed and slowly reversed out of the room. Why hadn't her mother sent her instead to her other grandfather's house, where you played all day and went out with a flask of coffee and sandwiches with Swart Piet and the cows? They were too mean in this house, and her mother had spoken to her sister already about the way she spoke to Sabah.

Shamila looked briefly in her direction, then put her foot down on the treadle, making the machine sing. Sabah liked the sounds it made. It reminded her of her mother at the sewing machine: the time when her father was gone for a week and she ran constantly into the house to check that her mother hadn't left too. But she didn't feel safe in this house. With seven boys next door calling her 'Whitey' in front of her friends, and her Granpa Doels with the cows and the sheep and lambs and those wonderful comic books living so far away.

'Let's go,' Moena said, taking a shiny sixpence out of her pocket. 'We have money for Stars. We can go to Abassie's on our way.'

'Okay.'

'Here's some toffee rolls,' Auntie Shamila said, reaching into her bag. 'Don't make yourselves all sticky, and come straight home, you hear?'

It was a three-mile walk to the white-plastered house next to the mosque, and the girls wasted all kinds of time in the store deciding between gumballs, Stars and Lucky Stripes. Sabah had left her toffee roll behind for that evening, when she would read the new book with the glossy pages Granpa Doels had dropped off for her, and took out her sixpence to contribute to the pool. Her mother didn't know of the two shillings she had in her drawer that Granpa Doels had given her when he showed up at school with Cadbury bars for her and her friends. He did things like that. Like the time when she was three and he bought her a pony and named it Masquerade, then started to call her that. 'Come here, my little Masquerade, read your ol' Granpa a story.' And she would lift the big book with the shiny cover to her knees and throw in some big words she'd heard on the radio. Her grandfather would laugh heartily and he'd go to the kitchen and whip them up bowls of blackberries with clotted cream. Or the time he invited her friends to stay with her at the farm during the school holidays and took them all to the gymkhana at Kenilworth and to the bioscope afterwards. She wished she could stay with him and Little Granny for good.

By the time they reached the calipha's house their faces were purple and pink, hands sticky, shoes scuffed from kicking pebbles and cans in the sluits.

'I'm scared,' Sabah said.

'Sheeda said it doesn't hurt.'

'They take off your panties,' Moena offered.

Julaiga giggled, and Sabah remembered that she wasn't wearing her navy blue knickers but the white nylon ones with the lace.

'They tickle you.'

'They don't tickle you, stupid. There's blood.'

'Blood?'

They stood at the gate looking up at the crowded stoep, the young girls wearing scarves, a woman in a black veil walking around with a plate.

'Is it a party?'

'They give you cake afterwards. Look, there's Soda. Let's go talk to her.'

'I'm not going,' Sabah said.

'You'll get a hiding if you don't.'

'Your mother can't hit me, she's not allowed.'

The woman with the cake plate waved them in.

On the stoep Sabah felt herself pressed in on all sides by girls pushing anxiously to go through the door into the house as if Father Christmas was on the other side. The ones coming out had a strange look, and some of them even smiled. Friends would huddle around, and the girl would lift up her dress and peer at her panties underneath. There would be whispering, giggling, the lady with the plate bringing tarts and ginger beer, everyone congratulating the girl as if she'd just won a prize.

'Did it hurt?' Moena asked Soda.

'No. Just a little prick.'

'Can we see the blood?'

'There's no blood.'

Moena turned to Sabah. 'See? I told you.'

She was in the living room now, fourth from the bedroom door. Why was she there? And when did these choky feelings start? She swallowed, trying to calm down. Was it at Oupa's funeral, or the time he told her father not to put his foot in the house again? She remembered it still. She was in bed in the front room, her father was on the stoep coming to take her mother back home. Oupa said no. 'She's not coming with you again.' She'd heard it all through the window, how he told her father to leave, her father's footsteps on the cement, the car starting up, the engine dying away down the street. How did her mother's father have the right to send her father away?

Looking at her cousins pushed up against her, she was breathing so fast, she passed out. When she opened her eyes, she was on a table with a light dangling over her legs, petrified by the black-veiled women holding her down, reaching under her dress: silent, toothless witches, reminding her of those birds with the long beaks sitting on dead animals in the bush.

She opened her mouth to scream, but nothing came out.

'Lookit de birdie,' one of them said, motioning to the fly-specked bulb overhead.

Sabah squeezed her knees together, but they were wrenched apart. She felt their clammy hands between her thighs. A sudden savageness rose in her breast. She wrenched her legs free, kicking at breasts and robes, knocking instruments to the floor. Six hands shot out, but her determination to escape was greater and she heard a savage scream pass her lips. Then she was at the door, cutting through bodies, snot catching in her brown strands, as she ran down the street.

Her mother had arrived to pick her up, and was in the kitchen drinking tea with her aunts. Charging past them to the back of the house, Sabah shot them venomous looks.

'Can't you greet? Even a dog barks,' Auntie Kareema said.

'No, I can't! And I won't! And you're not my mother!'

The women looked at one another. Her mother came to the bathroom door.

'Sabah? What's wrong, my girl? What happened? Where were you?'

Sabah didn't answer her. She turned on the tap in the bath and sat shivering on its edge. Her thighs were sticky and warm and, on her knee, a red tear sat in the groove of her skin. When she finally looked, she cried soundlessly into the hem of her dress to find her panties dry, and that whatever it was had only nicked the inside of her leg.

The pantie

Bongi was a few years old when she realised for the first time that the man in the suit and tie with the broken tooth who had come to visit her mother was her father. She knew this not by her mother's manner, for her mother hadn't smiled once since his arrival, but by the way Luthuli and MaJonasi, the people she and her mother lived with, fussed over him. He was the son working far away in the mines who came home once a year. She didn't like this man she had to call Father, the way he stood with his legs apart, his shoes shining like the glassiness of the river where her mother washed their clothes. He looked out of place in their hut, his laughter crude and a little loud. That night she lost her place next to her mother and had to sleep at the foot end of the bed. That night and for six nights after. When he left, her mother poured beer into a Vaseline jar, stuck it in a hole under the marula tree, and made her pleas to the ancestors. When it was full moon, she checked repeatedly between her legs, but there was nothing. She went to the old chief to throw the bones. The old chief wanted a goat. Her mother didn't have a goat. The eleven goats she came with now belonged to Luthuli and his wife. Everything belonged to the in-laws. In the end her mother crushed plants and made her own medicine. A few weeks later there was blood on the leaves and her mother was happy again.

Bongi saw him once more, a long, long time later, she didn't know how much later, she had no concept of time. No one could read or write or possessed calendars in KwaNgwanase, Natal. This time, when he came, her father stayed only three days. When he left, after hard words over money and another woman, her father's mother, MaJonasi, blamed her mother.

'You are bad, MiJsefa,' she railed. MiJsefa meant 'daughter of Joseph', and when MaJonasi was particularly frustrated with her daughter-in-law, she always started this way. 'You cannot keep a husband happy. You've chased my son away. What have you done to him? Don't you know how to keep a man? You do not know how to behave. Even when you speak to your father-in-law, you look directly into his eyes. We are Tsonga, not Zulu. Why my son married a Zulu, I don't know.'

Her mother said nothing. She never said anything. She washed and cooked and cleaned and took on all the insults like the layers and layers of fat creeping slowly up on her hips and thighs. It was no longer such a great ride on her mother's back, she was slow and heavy. Still, Bongi was her little girl. MiJsefa still carried her on long walks, still cleaned her bum with soft leaves, which she brought home and threw under the shadow of a tree so Bongi's spirit wouldn't be scattered all across Africa.

One day a woman came to the house and told her mother, 'Bongi must go to school.' The woman was angry with her mother.

'How old is she?'

'I don't know,' her mother said.

'And she's not wearing underwear. Where is her pantie? She's too big to be walking around like this.'

Her mother had looked at the woman, surprised, then ashamed. The woman had nodded her head irritably. She was coming the next day to take Bongi to school. That afternoon her mother did no work in the field. She emptied the mealie sack of its contents and sat with a needle in her hand and made Bongi a new dress. She made it to her knees so no one could see underneath. The first thing the woman did when she arrived in the morning was look under the dress. She said nothing to her mother, but it was obvious she was upset.

At the school there was some argument with a teacher about Bongi coming too late, it was March already, almost the end of the term. She had missed too much, she must come next year. The woman insisted and the school took her in. Bongi liked this woman. She was younger than her mother, with a narrow back, her skin the colour of thick cream. She had never seen a white woman before. The woman held her hand tightly, and seemed unafraid of anyone. Bongi vowed that she would be like this woman when she was big. This woman would never fatten with the insults of old men.

School was five miles from home. In the mornings Bongi walked with two other girls from her village. In the afternoons, her mother waited for her under the tree on the other side of the road. MiJsefa would take out a thick slice of bread and a bottle of water, and they would eat before making the long trip home. Bongi no longer rode on her back.

'And what have you learned today?' her mother asked one afternoon.

'The letters of the alphabet. I know all of them.'

'Soon you will be able to read and write. One day you can write some letters for me. Do you play with the other girls?'

'Only some games. Not skipping.'

'Why not?'

'When the girls jump, you can see everything. They all wear panties. White ones. Some of them with flowers on it. If I jump, they will see that I am not wearing anything.'

MiJsefa was silent the rest of the way. When they arrived home, she slaughtered a chicken she had saved for a special occasion, and presented her in-laws with the roasted legs for their evening meal. When they had finished eating, she asked Luthuli, careful to avoid his eyes and speaking in a most humble tone, if he could lend her two rand. She would repay this when her sister visited in winter. The flowers in the field were all fading, it wouldn't be long before the rains came.

'What is this money for?'

'I have to buy underwear for Bongi. The girls in school — '

He didn't let her finish. 'Bongi doesn't have need for fancy underwear. If she must have it, make her one out of a mealie sack.'

Bongi watched in shame as her mother picked up the dishes and went to wash them outside. Her mother never asked them for anything again. Even when she knew a letter had come from Jo'burg from her father to Luthuli and a neighbour was called in to read it, she never asked what was in it. Bongi was sure that this bothered MaJonasi more than anything, because for weeks the letter lay around the hut and her mother dusted around it, over it, under it, but never asked anything about it.

The day following her father-in-law's stinginess with the two rand, her mother waited for her at the school gate after school instead of at her usual spot across the street, and said she wanted to speak to the teacher. The teacher listened to her request, and said the school was just two rooms and a toilet, there was no telephone. But he gave her change with which to make a call at Moola's Café in the village. There, in front of hordes of people crowding the small shop, her mother begged the owner for the use of his telephone. Mr Moola said he wasn't a post office. He didn't like customers coming behind his counter. Was she going to buy anything in the shop? How long would she talk? Where was the call to? By the time her mother held the receiver in her hand, she was sweating. She did not talk long. Five or six sentences. When they were out of the shop, MiJsefa told her that her auntie would visit in a few weeks. Before the new term started, Bongi would have her underwear.

Bongi knew the days of the week, when school would end, when the new term would begin. Every night she went to bed hoping that the next day would see her auntie coming over the veld. Her mother had only one sister, Auntie MaKhumalo, who visited a few times during the year, sometimes staying four and five days when her husband was away working, the three of them sharing the small bed. Auntie MaKhumalo never came empty-handed and usually there was a packet of Marie Biscuits, and a handful of toffees.

Bongi considered putting the beer jar under the marula tree for the izinyanya, to see if they could make her auntie come faster, but the rains had started and she had no desire to sit outside in the mud. Besides, she had little faith in her mother's ancestors. They had not once provided money, or clothes, or good health, or any of the other things her mother begged and prayed for under the tree. Perhaps they were just good listeners and only helpful for marriages and births, which required nothing more than a happy silence. Or perhaps they had to change the tree under which all the appealing went on. Why did it have to be a marula and not some other kind? What would happen if her mother put the jar in a hole under a mahogany tree and did her beseeching there? Still, she was happy with the outcome of the call, and had visions of the pantie her auntie would bring, how it would feel against her skin, what colour. She hoped it was white. Two of the girls had white underwear, and when they jumped it was such a thing of beauty against their dark skin.

The end of the school term arrived, and still no auntie came. But, one morning suddenly, towards the end of the holidays, there was Auntie MaKhumalo in her best skirt and shoes, sitting talking with her mother outside on a tree stump when Bongi woke up. There was the usual surprise over how much Bongi had grown, then her auntie opened the small bundle tucked inside a bigger bundle in her cloth bag. 'Bongi, Bongi, your Auntie MaKhumalo has brought you something special.' With great pride, she took out the gift.

Bongi knelt at her feet with gratitude. She turned it this way and that, a soft, snowy white nylon pantie with the 99-cent label still attached. She ran inside and fitted it on. And promptly sat down and cried. She had never owned anything new, never felt anything so soft and beautiful against her skin. It was the first thing she owned that was bought from a store. Even her doll was a dried mealie cob, the hair plaited leaves, the legs made out of sticks. There was no mirror in the hut, so she looked down at herself, test-ing the elastic around her thin thighs with her fingers, caressing the label. Then she took it off and shook it out. She would not wear the pantie until school started. She wanted it to be brand new when she wore it the first time.

The first Monday morning of the new term arrived. There was no need for MiJsefa to wake her up. Bongi had brought water from the river the night before and kept it in a basin under the bed where no one could take it for coffee or tea. She washed her face and scrubbed between her legs. Then put on the pantie.

'You will take it off when you come home from school,' her mother said, 'and don't forget to wash there before you put it on.'

That day it rained and everyone stayed indoors during the first break. When she got home in the afternoon, Bongi looked wearily out from the hut, wondering when the weather would change. But it rained three more days, and every day she came home, took off her pantie, shook it out, and laid it flat on the box on her mother's cupboard. Even though she washed herself vigorously between the legs, she noticed a stiffness and smell in the crotch. But she couldn't wash it. Her mother had said not to do so more than once every two weeks; the pantie had to last until the end of Sub A.

On Friday the sun came out and dried all the puddles in the schoolyard. One of the girls in her class, Evelyn, brought out the skipping rope.

'Who wants to play skipping?'

'I do, I do,' Bongi said quickly.

'But you never play skipping with us. Can you skip?'

'Yes.'

'Okay. I'll go first. Then Mary. Then you.'

Bongi took one end of the rope, Mary the other, and the game was under way. Evelyn and Mary were good skippers and Bongi waited a long time for them to finish. When it was finally her turn to step into the swing of the rope, a gang of girls had gathered around. Bongi hadn't played skipping for a long time, and as she jumped to the rhythm of the beat of the rope as it slapped into the red gravel, she took care not to let it get caught in her feet.

'I didn't know you could skip like this,' Mary said, her arm getting tired.

'Me, too,' Evelyn said. 'You tricked us.'

Bongi wasn't listening. She had visualised this moment since the first week of school. Jumping higher and higher, the mealie-sack dress sliding up and down her thighs, her thoughts were entirely focused on lifting her feet. Could they see it? Could they see the whiteness of it, the label, and how much it cost?

The doekoem

I was on my knees in front of the kitchen dresser, unpacking jam, condensed milk, lentils and beans, removing the oil cloth, wiping the area with a soapy rag, squeezing water into an enamel basin – a job I had Friday afternoons after school, as well as polishing the brass and shining up the mirrors in the house – when there was a mouse-like patter and a knock and Patty's face appeared at the kitchen door.

Patty Gonzales lived with her married sister down the street, and had taken to coming to my grandmother since that time her baby had burned with a fever and Oemie had made an instant diagnosis, going outside for the stem of a plant, inserting the crushed tip into the baby's behind. The baby went blue as he howled, seconds later a brown jet shooting from his bum.

'There!' Oemie exclaimed, 'packed fulla shit as I thought,' washing her hands, donating the last squash from the pantry for the baby's supper that night. There was never any food at Patty's house. And here was Patty again, Simon on her hip, her stomach bigger than the last time.

My grandmother had been shelling peas and drew her huge body out of the chair, wrapping her long scarf tightly about her hair, rolling the ends into coils, then weaving it in under the over-lapped edges.

'Come in, Patty. Long time no see.'

'Yes, Mrs Abrahams,' Patty laughed nervously. 'How is Mrs Abrahams?'

'Fine, with the grace of God. Just the leg hurts now and then, you know, when it rains. Are you having another baby, Patty?'

Patty took the seat offered, and as soon as she sat down, started to cry over Simon's curly head.

I knew what was next: Sabah, go play in the other room. Sabah, go do the mirrors in the lounge. *Walls have ears, you know.*

'Go see if the postman came. Your mummy's expecting some letters.'

'He came this morning, Oemie.'

'Well, take an iceblock and go play outside, then.'

I threw the dirty water in the sink, took a raspberry iceblock from the freezer tray, and ran out before she remembered the other jobs.

But I was interested in what had brought Patty again – there was sure to be a story – so I ran out the front, and crept around the side of the house. Licking the red drops dripping down my arm onto my elbow, I sat on my heels outside the kitchen window next to the drain.

'… a terrible thing …', Patty's voice drifted out. 'I wonder if Mrs Abrahams can perhaps help me.'

It was amazing how many people came to my grandmother for help. If it wasn't for ointment for a rotten sore, for jam and bread, bus fare, advice, it was for favours way out of line. One night my mother returned from work to find a dead man laid out in the living room. The man, a Muslim friend of a neighbour who said the dead man had no relatives, had died of a stroke, and my grandmother, feeling sorry for the neighbour who said he didn't know anything about Muslim funerals, offered to take it on. My mother arrived to a house smelling of incense and kifaaitkos – 'funeral food' made with mutton, carrots and peas – and filled with strangers who'd come to pay their respects, my grandmother floating about in her black robes directing the show. My mother had to stand all night serving tea, the next day scrubbing and spraying with Beattie to get the smell of camphor and dead body out. Beattie could do the washing and polishing and make up beds, but Beattie wasn't allowed to touch my Friday jobs. 'We want you to do these things yourself, so you'll know how to run your own house one day.'

'I came to Mrs Abrahams because I thought perhaps Mrs Abrahams know of someone I can go to.'

'Go to? What kind of someone?'

Patty cleared her throat.

'What kind of someone, Patty?'

'A doekoem, Mrs Abrahams.'

'A doekoem?' I heard the shock in my grandmother's voice. The only thing I knew about doekoems was what I'd overheard at my aunt's house. They were people with funny eyes and strange powers and could do great favours if you did what they asked and stayed on their good side. Auntie Kareema's friend, who was 40 already, had gone to one, and in no time was married to a man she'd fancied, who'd walked past her at the bus stop for two years without paying her any attention.

'I don't go to doekoems, Patty. Muslims don't believe in such things.'

'I just thought perhaps if Mrs Abrahams know someone. Doris says — '

'What do you want to go to a doekoem for? They just take your money, it doesn't work.'

There was a short silence during which the kettle was plunked on the stove.

'Does Mrs Abrahams remember Issy Sulaiman?'

'The one who did the deed, and afterwards you didn't see his dust? I remember that rotter, yes. What about him?'

'There was reasons, Mrs Abrahams. His family would've never accepted me, being an Apostolic and all.'

'You make too many excuses for that boy, Patty.'

'He came back,' Patty continued. 'After Simon was born. We talk 'n' talk and he said he wanted us to be a family.'

'Well, that's something.'

'I was going to convert and change my name to Latiefah and we were gonna get married by Muslim rites by that imam in Athlone. He said he would burn in Hell if he turned – Muslims don't turn for Christians.'

'He should've thought of Hell when he had you under him. And?'

'He bought those little books from the mosque, and I met Imam Patel. I spoke to my mother, and she said — '

'What happened, Patty? Get to the point.'

My grandmother's a woman of little patience – no frills 'n' drills, as she calls it – and I could imagine the right eyebrow higher than the left.

'I got pregnant again, Mrs Abrahams. As Mrs Abrahams can see. When I told him, he never came back.'

'Are you surprised, Patty?'

'A man can't do all this with a woman and not care, Mrs Abrahams.'

'Don't talk to me about what a man can do, Patty. When that iron's standing stiff between his legs he's not thinking of anything.'

'But he loves me, Mrs Abrahams. I know.'

'Love?' my grandmother laughed. 'Don't be getting your head full of that tommy-rot. Love's for movie stars who marry four and

five times and have to call it something. Forget about love. You can't
think of love with one on your lap and one coming on. The right
man will come when the time's right.'

'He's the father, Mrs Abrahams,' Patty cried. 'I don't wanna be
alone.'

'You know, Patty, some women love to hurt. Any feeling is better than no feeling at all. Even if it kicks them in the gut. Let old
Mrs Abrahams teach you something today. I'm not an educated
woman, but there's one thing I've learned being with Mr
Abrahams for 40 years. You *are* alone, my girl. You arrive alone and
you leave alone. No one gets into the box with you when you die.
Husbands come and go, children leave. Before you can depend on
a man, you must be able to depend on yourself. We all want to feel
safe. Especially us women who think we can't breathe without a
man next to us in bed. But safety doesn't come from a man, Patty,
it comes from you. You know what I'm saying? Go to church. Think
about your children, get a job. If you don't mind me saying, that
boy's not going to marry you. Not because of religion, that's an
excuse. I don't want to be cruel, Patty, but the snake's been in the
bush – if you know the ending, why buy the book?'

Patty's crying started up again.

'There you go, Patty. Alles sal regkom. All will be well.'

'Will Mrs Abrahams not marry again?'

'Me? No, Patty. The pistons are old and worn out, I don't have
the stomach for another man. There, have some biscuits and tea
and don't waste any more tears on that Issy.'

Patty left soon after with a carrier bag of greens, promising to
follow Oemie's advice. I thought that the end of the matter.

Three weeks later Patty was back.

'Mrs Abrahams, can I talk to Mrs Abrahams for a minute?'

'Yes, Patty, come in.'

'He came again last night out of the blue. Can Mrs Abrahams see what he's doing? He's very sorry, he said. His mother was sick, that's why he couldn't come. He wants to make things right. Clean up his mess, he said. I don't wanna believe him, but I'm going to, Mrs Abrahams.'

'And that's your right. You know best what's good for you. But he couldn't call to tell you his mother was sick?'

'He had lots of things on his mind, he said. But I came to Mrs Abrahams, because I still have that favour to ask. I still wanna see someone. Mrs Abrahams know what I mean?'

'I told you, Patty — '

'Before he changes his mind again.'

'But if he changes his mind again, it's better for you to know now – don't you see?'

'Please, if Mrs Abrahams can help me out just this one time.'

'How, Patty? I told you I don't — '

'Doris said Mrs Abrahams knows someone in Retreat. Mrs Abrahams took her Ralphie there when he had that curse on him and he kept getting into accidents.'

Oemie finally noticed me at the table pretending to read my school books.

'Don't listen to old people's conversations. Go and play outside.'

I went to the same spot under the kitchen window, and listened in.

'... it's a long time ago since I took Doris to see that man, I don't know. And Doris shouldn't be talking of such things. If my daughter found out, there'll be oorlog in this house.'

'Please, Mrs Abrahams. I can get a car to take us. We don' have to be long.'

My grandmother was notorious for bothering neighbours for

lifts, and I thought it smart of Patty to bring up the availability of a car.

'Let me think about it. It'll have to be Monday or Tuesday, during the day. I don't believe in these things, Patty, you can't mess with the Will of God. But if we go, the man charges ten rand. Bring twelve just in case. I don't think it'll work. One can't believe in God and these things at the same time. What kind of a believer will that make me? People can't perform miracles. Only God.'

On Monday, when I returned from school, Oemie was wearing her black cloak over a beige dress, and a cream veil, her eyes darkened with kohl. This was her only vanity, and a handsome woman my grandmother was with her skin the colour of a copper penny, her medorah flecked with gold. When you saw the kohl and smelled the eau-de-cologne, you knew you were going somewhere.

A peanut butter sandwich waited for me on the kitchen table, and I had hardly had time to take off my school uniform when the hooter of the car sounded outside.

'Come, come,' she rushed me out the door. 'We have to be back by five.' And shouting back at Beattie, who was seeing us off, 'That meat's almost soft, Beattie. Put the potatoes in and turn the stove off in half an hour.'

Beattie was good at a lot of things, but once she started listening to those afternoon serials, her brain switched off. My grandmother was taking a helluva chance with my mother's supper that night.

The car took us through side streets and avenues all the way past the race track, up the Main Road, down more streets until, twenty minutes later, we arrived in a grey little strip lined with council homes. Snot-nosed children played in the street, unafraid of oncoming cars, dogs shitting right next to the older children playing transistor radios on the pavement.

'Did you bring something that belongs to him?' my grand-mother asked.

'Yes.'

'And don't look in the man's eye.'

'What's wrong with his eye?'

'He's blind, I think, but I'm not sure. Don't look just in case he can see. It's not good to be mixed up with people like this, Patty. This is the only time and the last time.'

The driver stopped at a house with a sad-looking flower in a jam tin in the window, a beat-up beige Renault on cement blocks right on the small patch of sand supposed to be the front lawn.

My grandmother looked at me sitting in the back seat. 'You'd better come in with us.'

Did she think I was going to remain in the car?

The ground was wet from the rain and my school walkers squished in the mud. An old woman asked us in, pointing to a dimly lit kitchen at the back.

The house was damp, with the odours of an animal barn, and I automatically dipped my nose behind my shirt collar, trying not to breathe. The curtains were drawn, even in the tiny living room we passed through, where another lady sat mending clothes in the half-dark. I felt suddenly hot and tight like the time at the Cango Caves with Granpa Doels when I had crawled into a small space and for an instant was paralysed, imagining the mountain collaps-ing on me into the ground.

In the kitchen a dirty bulb hung from the ceiling over a red, metal-edged formica table, four chairs squeezed into the small space where two heavily made-up ladies in pressed blouses and skirts, probably customers, looked very out of place. Even more out of place was the scraggly goat not three feet from their buckled brogues, the rope around his neck hooked to the nail in the back door. The air reeked of boiled tripe and wet goat.

There was nowhere to sit, and I leaned against the back of my grandmother's chair, not knowing where to let my eyes fall. They strayed briefly to the cracked lino on the floor and the Primus stove and cooldrink crate under the table, resting finally on the goat eyeing me warily from under two nasty horns. I had an uncontrollable urge to run.

'Oemie? I have to pee.'

'Didn't I tell you to pee before you go out?'

'I forgot.'

'Go ask the old lady in the front where the lavvy is.'

'I'll come with you,' Patty said.

'People off the street have the nerve to use it,' the old woman said, 'so it's a little blocked. There's newspaper under a stone by the door.'

The smell hit me when we rounded the house, and I despaired when I saw the wooden contraption with the hanging door, big puddles out in front.

'I can't go in, Patty. It stinks.'

Patty was anxious to get back to the house.

'There's no one around. Why don't I stand here, and you pee behind the lavvy?'

There was no sign of paper under a stone, and what was flying about in the yard was wet and soiled.

'Do you have any tissues?'

Patty looked in her bag. 'No. Just pee, and shake it off.'

The thought of squatting out in the open, in front of a stranger, the cold wind hitting my behind, made me wish Patty had kept her problems to herself. But I felt the first drops squeeze out. Squatting quickly behind the lavatory, I peed on my shoe.

'I need some paper, Patty.'

Patty looked in her bag again, and still couldn't come up with anything. Then she lifted up her skirt, and tore off a piece of petticoat.

I took the nylon square, spat on it, then wiped myself, washing my hands at the tap, dabbing cold water on my contaminated foot.

'We're next,' my grandmother said when we returned to find the fancy ladies gone. 'Wait here in the kitchen, we won't be long.'

'I don't want to sit here with the goat, Oemie.'

'What are you scared of? That goat won't do anything. Well, come on, then.'

The old lady showed us into the bedroom and closed the door. If I thought the house scary, the dwarf on the pink candlewick bedspread in the hole of a room with its magazine cut-out of a sad Jesus Christ on a green wall and a half-revealed pee pot under the bed struck new fear in my heart. Dark, with wiry hair, the doekoem was crippled and deformed, with white cataracts on his eyes. His head moved when we came in, nostrils twitching as he sniffed at the air.

'En wie kom hier?'

'Mrs Abrahams. Van Steurhof.'

He thought for a moment. 'Ooh, Mrs Abrahams. Die kind met die krippel been.'

'Daai's reg. Mnr Poggenpoel het 'n goeie memory.'

'What bring you today, missies?'

'I got someone with me.'

'I know.'

'She's got a problem with a man.'

The old man waited.

'Patty?' my grandmother prodded. 'Speak up.'

Patty seemed mesmerised by the doekoem, but launched into a long speech, dabbing occasionally at the spit in the corner of her

mouth. When she was done, ending with a long sigh, she waited
for the miracle.

'Better to leave some things as they are,' the doekoem said without turning his head. 'If Mrs Abrahams understand.' He didn't
speak directly to Patty.

'I told her, but you know how these young people are.'

'Did she bring a piece of his clothes?'

'I got one of his ties,' Patty said, bringing it out of her bag.

The doekoem took it from her and threw it on the cold cement
floor between the two single beds where we sat. Then he took a
stick as gnarled as himself and poked it into the maroon material,
stirring it around on the floor like a witch stirring a brew. I'd seen
the movie with Moses, and expected to see the tie wriggle and
raise its head.

'I see him coming,' the doekoem said.

'What do you mean?' Patty asked.

'I see him coming over.'

How could he see Issy the scoundrel when he couldn't see us,
I wondered.

The stirring continued. 'But he needs work.'

'You see him coming to me?' Patty asked.

'Yes. But — '

'What?'

'Ssshh. Let the man do his work,' my grandmother said.

For a woman who said she didn't believe in such things, she
was very curious about Mr Poggenpoel's findings on the dirty
floor.

'I want to know the problem, Mrs Abrahams,' Patty said. 'Maybe
if I know the problem, I can fix it.'

The stirring stopped, and just when I thought the doekoem had
fallen asleep and forgotten us, he spoke.

'There's a woman.'

'A woman? It can't be.'

'A woman with long hair.'

'He's got another woman? I don't believe it.' She turned to look at my grandmother. My grandmother gave her a look that said, I told you the man was a rotter. I'd heard that word 'rotter' many times.

'I didn't say so. I just said there's a woman.'

'Can Mr Poggenpoel help me then?' Patty was desperate.

'I can give you someting for him. It will bring him over to you.'

'Really? What?'

'Some special water. When you get home, find a bottle to put it in. Make it look like a present and give it to him. It's important that nothing happens to this bottle. That bottle stays with him seven days, he's yours.'

'Can I put the water in his tea? Just to make sure?'

'The water's from a dassie's pee. If you drink it, it does someting else.'

'What if the bottle breaks — '

'It mustn't.'

'Or gets lost?'

The doekoem got up to indicate the visit was over.

We left there at five thirty with water in a fishpaste jar, Oemie panicking at the late hour.

'Don't let me hear you repeat any of this,' she said, handing me a pink sweet not to tell my mother where we'd been.

We didn't see Patty again until the summertime, and then it was at the ticket counter at Steurhof station, where Patty had just got off the train we had to take into town. Simon had grown, and was holding onto her dress, the new baby in Patty's arms.

'Patty, I haven't seen you in months. Where've you been?'

'I got me a job as a machinist in Salt River,' Patty said. 'Four days a week. My sister looks after them while I work.'

'And Issy?' I was as anxious as my grandmother to know about the rotter.

Patty's voice made a funny sound. 'Ag, Mrs Abrahams.'

My grandmother waited.

'Mrs Abrahams was maar right.'

'What do you mean, Patty? Don't go so round 'n' round.'

'It didn't work.'

'What happened?'

'The cashier at Easy-Kleen in Wynberg, Mrs Abrahams. He didn't even wait for the child to be born. He got right in bed with that Indian bitch.'

'What do you mean?'

'That night when I gave him the bottle as the doekoem said, he put it in his jacket pocket. We had supper at a takeout and some curry fell on the lapel. The next day he took the jacket to the cleaners and the bottle was still in it.'

'Oh, my word.'

'The cashier, Mr Karjieker's daughter: Mrs Abrahams know the one with the long, greasy plait? She served him, and from that day on, Mrs Abrahams, I dunno what got into him, but he never came back.'

The tale was long and pitiful, my grandmother forgetting all about the man waiting for us in Wynberg. We missed two trains, and ended up walking back home with Patty carrying her bags and the baby.

The middle children

Smartly dressed in knee-high boots, miniskirt, Beatles jacket and black beret, Sabah got off the bus at Mowbray station and walked down the steps into the subway to the other side. Passing the thick knot of commuters who had bottled out of the bus to the far side of the platform where the first-class passengers would board, she was nervous, as always, expecting to hear her name called. The bus had loaded most of its fares in Athlone, and one day someone would shout her name, and the charade would end.

The two-minute wait for the train was the worst.

Turning to the crossword in the *Times*, she looked at the other travellers: the Carnaby girl with the op art earrings chewing gum, the heavy-set Afrikaner with the folded *Burger*, the bell-bottomed hairdresser from Scissors 'n Things – she'd seen his picture advertised – and the other girl standing by herself at the far end of the platform.

The other girl was like herself. Not white, not black, but the off-spring of many races: the middle child of a dysfunctional womb. She knew about the other girl as she knew the other girl knew about her. As a denture-wearer knows another plastic smile, an afflicted middle child could tell. From the stance, the wariness in the eyes. A middle child's constant fear was to be tapped on the shoulder and told to go to the section reserved for non-whites.

The train arrived and she got on. Rocking gently in the green leather seat to the familiar rhythms of the carriage, blending in with the pressed suits and crisp linens, she returned to her anagrams. Then something made her look up. Stephanie van Niekerk from South Peninsula High! She hadn't seen Steffie since she took up with the German designer with the green MG and moved into his flat in Green Point. Fair, with lots of freckles and sheets of raven-black hair, Stephanie had a ballerina's prance, flicking her hair when she walked.

They got up from their seats and met near the door where there was standing room.

'Sabah!'

'Howzit?'

They were not suprised to find each other in this front section of the train.

'I heard you'd gone to Germany.'

'I did. We came back.'

'For good?'

'Yes. We live in Newlands now.'

Good old Newlands, Sabah thought. Serene and green, and no hawkers allowed.

'I'm still with Wolfie, you know,' Stephanie continued.

'Really? That's quite a long time. It's working out then?'

'Yes. And Laine's still with Joachim. They've got two kids now.'

'And your other sisters? How many were there again?'

'Five. All married except for Janey, who got divorced. She's always had bad luck with guys. And you? I don't see a ring.'

'Ah, well.'

Steffie's eyes twinkled. 'You're moving with the wrong crowd.'

Sabah laughed.

'Get yourself a German or a Swede, Sabah. I'm telling you. They don't have that coloured mentality, and they like dark. They come here because they're attracted to the exotic look.'

'Maybe if I wasn't Muslim I could.'

'Could what?'

'You know, try white.'

Stephanie laughed. 'You still have all those religious hang-ups?'

'I'm full of them.'

'Shame.'

'Don't shame me, it's not that bad. I got engaged last year.'

'Really?'

'We were going to leave for Canada. I called it off. I don't want to leave South Africa. He's in Vancouver now.'

'Shame.'

'Stop it.'

'Well, Wolfgang and I also have plans. We want to start a family.'

Sabah smiled. Stephanie's life had worked out. With a German husband, she'd have fair children, they'd attend a white school and start out on the right foot. But could Stephanie escape who she was? Could you take a born-again pill with your Milo and wake up someone else?

'You must come to the house. Wolfie has some terrific friends. Maybe you'll like Kurt. His English isn't very good, but he's blond with blue eyes and a programmer with IBM. He doesn't have a girlfriend right now. How about tomorrow night? We can meet under the clock and take the train home together after work. There're always people coming over, you never know who you can meet.'

At Cape Town station she watched Stephanie in her strapless heels walk towards the Foreshore, strangely curious at the prospect of Friday night. Would she be enticed? Did she envy Steffie's world? It was sure to be more exciting than hers. Things were easier as a

Christian. You could marry anyone. She'd once had a crush on a boy in Standard Six, Brian Dreyer, but even as a twelve-year-old she knew that she couldn't entertain it. She wasn't anything like her friend. The first to smoke, experiment with sex, cross the colour line, Stephanie would laugh if she knew Sabah was still a virgin at twenty-one.

'A Sergeant van Schalkwyk's been calling for you,' the receptionist said when she reached work. 'He says he's with the CID.'

'The CID?' What would Criminal Investigations want with her? She went to her desk, and called the number.

'Miss Solomon,' a heavily accented voice said, 'we'd like you to come down to Caledon Street Police Station this morning if you can.'

'Is something wrong?' Her heart trilled in her chest.

'We have information that you're using a white card.'

Her breath caught in her throat. 'What do you mean?'

There was irritation in his voice. 'You were reported, we know you have a white card.'

'Reported? By who?'

'Can you come down this morning, please?'

Sabah put down the phone and called her father. Why she had called him, she didn't know. She lived with her mother. Her father was someone she saw sporadically over the holidays. She had never called him for anything.

Her father came with his lawyer, Jeffrey Fine, and met her outside the police station. Her father was a character himself. When she was born, he refused to have her registered, her mother said. And himself refused to endorse any card labelling him. 'He can be rude, your father. He's not afraid of anyone. The only man he had any respect for was his father. I met him once, in our kitchen in Lincoln Estate. Your father never said it was his father, but I knew he was. He's a Jew, you know. Your surname would've been Abrahams.'

But who would've reported her, she wondered.

'Leave the talking to me,' the lawyer said.

There were two of them, one with friendly eyes, acting graciously, setting her at ease, the other one asking the pointed questions. The tea girl came in with a tray, and Van Schalkwyk offered them a cup.

De Wet came straight to the point.

'It's a serious offence to obtain a white identification card if you're not white, Miss Solomon.'

The lawyer stepped in. 'My client doesn't deny that she has a card. But we'd like you to take some things into account, why she did it. Sabah's a respectable girl from an educated family, white in appearance, and obtained the card because — '

'We're not talking about sitting in white restaurants or bio-scopes, Mr Fine. We can all see she can pass. She broke the law and we can't get away from that.'

'There were no business schools five years ago for non-whites and Sabah obtained the card when she was sixteen to get into TBI. It was only a means to enhance her skills. And she's made some-thing of herself. She's a legal assistant now. She knows what she's done's against the law, and has panic attacks worrying about being found out. She didn't get the card to be white, but for some of the small privileges we take for granted. It's not a crime, Sergeant, to want to leap some of the hurdles in life.'

'You're right, Mr Fine, we're parents ourselves, we all want the best for our kids. But there're laws in this country, and we can't have people just helter-skelter breaking them. Now, we understand that she's applied to Canada for a visa and has received one.'

Her father interjected. 'That was last year. She's not interested in emigrating anymore.'

'So we're prepared to negotiate,' Van Schalkwyk continued, as if no one had spoken. 'The names of the people who supplied the card, and she's free to leave the country. No charges will be brought. She has to be gone within a month.'

'What?'

'That's the deal,' De Wet said.

'But that's outrageous!'

'Life's outrageous, Mr Fine. We're being generous. The names of the people or organisation who supplied the card, and gone by the end of next month. It's not that we don't want her in South Africa, South Africa belongs to all of us, but if she's not here when we make the arrests, we can't put her in jail, can we?'

Fine talked back and forth for two hours, but it was like pissing into Victoria Falls. Sabah sat listening. How could she tell them that she'd had nothing to do with getting the card, and that she hadn't even been consulted? Her mother had just wanted to give her a chance.

Van Schalkwyk closed the file and got up. 'We'll leave you for a few minutes to sort yourselves out.'

Fine was brutally frank. The Security Police were not to be underestimated. She would be made an example of, her picture would appear in the papers, and there was the possibility of jail. Was Canada not worth a try? He himself had friends there. It was a chance for a better life.

De Wet and Van Schalkwyk returned, and Fine made a last desperate plea. The sergeants sat unmoving. With the cold speed of a bank transaction, the name of the contact – deceased two years previously – was given, and Sabah was released.

On a dismal day in May, her mother's Crimplene dress a white dot on the dock, Table Mountain bid her a silent goodbye. The wind whipped at her hair and she sank down between the passengers and cried into her hands.

I count the bullets
sometimes

I reckon before I tell you about Jeremy Vosloo, I should start with two years ago, the year the blacks started protesting against the use of Afrikaans in their schools in Soweto and the protests grew into riots, setting off a wave of demonstrations spreading throughout the country until it arrived ugly and angry in Cape Town, and my father had this bright idea to send me to private school. He always had these bright ideas, my father – from the brooders and turkey-cocks he brought home one Saturday afternoon in a cage in the back of the bakkie, declaring that we no longer had to buy eggs from Mr Doep, the chicken pen eventually growing into a caco-phony of red-combed birds snapping at your heels and no one col-lecting the eggs or raking up; to the sheep and goats and a stubborn ewe charging all the visitors. My father, you see, had grown up one of nine sons in a box in District Six, and had dreamed of a backyard where he could swing his arms without knocking into his neighbour's lavatory. When his clothing factory landed this big account, taking fashion stores from Cape Town to Mafeking, we moved from a comfortable house on the slopes of Walmer Estate, where there was life and civilisation, to this remote place in Philippi he likes to call the farm.

Now, despite all the complaints after the lorry pulled away with our things – the old place had been too cramped, too high on the hill, the hot-water cylinder didn't hold enough – there was something about that Ravenscraig Road beauty, all highly polished oak smelling of lavender wax and my grandmother's crunchy pine-nut tameletjies, that was hard to resist. It was the kind of house where you could run through from front door to kitchen and out the back in four seconds flat and travel years, with all the history and life steeped in those high beams and plastered walls. And that's another thing. Even my illiterate grandmother, sitting with her huge bum on our folded pyjamas, pressing them on the stoep, eating raspberry iceblocks with condensed milk with Sies Galima from across the street, needed some kind of excitement to survive, and refused to come with us, moving in with my uncle down the street.

In any event, my father had bought this plot, called in contractors and landscape artists and, with the blessings of Barclays Bank, produced for his family a Cape Dutch-style home, with oak doors and curved fanlights and brass knobs, velvet lawns, stables, servants' quarters, a kidney-shaped pool, and a pack of trained Dobermans. The fantasy was started and all sorts of animals began to arrive. The problem was, the more animals came, the more people were hired, and my father worked harder, not getting to enjoy the smell of all this warm chicken shit. So when he pushed his *Argus* aside one night, looking at my mother – who was the real boss of the house – and broke the news that I was starting at a boys' high school in Bishopscourt, I wondered if he'd gone mad. My cousin Rudwan already said we lived like we thought we'd been born in the saddle when not one of us had raised a leg over a filly, and here he was setting me farther apart. Private school, I argued, was for those coloureds salivating through plate-glass windows at the world of the whites. Didn't I already read the news in the *Argus* every night? Wasn't my English better than my sisters'?

But I really should start with that first day, my mother driving me in the silver Benz, depositing me, new satchel and all, in front of this school with hundreds of green-blazered boys on the grounds, the only snoekie in a sea of yellowtail. I knew I was in the right class when I saw my name on the board, and in the wrong school when I stood by myself during break. I cursed my parents. How could they do this to me when I could've been with Rudwan at Sinton High?

I noticed this boy with platinum hair and a cowlick, a garden snake in his hand, chasing after a fat student called Albert Mostert, who was clearly horrified. Albert's short legs carried him chop-chop to the principal's office, where Jeremy got a warning and was quickly relieved of his pet. Sitting three seats behind them in the biology class, I watched Jeremy look furtively behind him, take a chameleon out of his pocket, and put it down Albert's neck. Albert jumped up with a scream and Mr Greaves dropped the chalk he was busy writing with at the blackboard, demanding the name of the culprit. Jeremy looked about as curious as the rest of the class to see who could've done such a thing. It looked like I'd found a friend.

That weekend Rudwan visited, and watched from the safe side of the henhouse while I waded through a gang of angry birds collecting eggs for a neighbour, my tackies crunching in the grey and white shit. I mean, were we an eggerama or something that we had to supply the neighbourhood? We ate so many things made with eggs – puddings, omelettes, soufflés – that you could probably pull the animal fat in thick worms from our veins. The pittance charged didn't even cover the chicken-feed.

'I'm in the swimming team,' I said to him.

'There's a pool?'

'And a tennis court and pingpong room.'

He hung his head, and the zing went out of the brag. 'But they're too strict, you can't even chew gum on the school grounds.'

'You're joking.'

'And don't let them catch you wearing your uniform after school on the street. They also have this stupid rule that if a teacher comes down the stairs, you have to stop and let him pass, and say "Good morning, sir," or "Afternoon, sir," and not move until he does.'

'That's stupid. Sinton hasn't got sturvy rules like that, and you can eat and chew what you want. Did you make any friends?'

'Yes.'

'Who?'

'Jeremy Vosloo.'

'A boer?'

'Dunno. You want to go catch tadpoles after I take in the eggs?'

We went out with our jars, but it wasn't the same as before. At supper my sisters, taking advantage of Rudwan's presence and my father's good mood, made their own charges.

'I don't see why he gets to go to private school when we have to go around here,' Layla, my second youngest sister complained. 'He gets everything.'

'Shut up, Layla. You're only in Standard Two.'

'I won't shut up. You get so much things just 'cause you're a boy.'

'So many things.'

'Stop correcting everyone. And keep quiet both of you,' my mother warned.

'Layla's right. I'm going to high school next year. Will it be private school, too?' Soraya asked.

'We'll see your marks in June.'

My father waited for his youngest child, but Ruby was too busy sucking on the bone of her chop. Ruby didn't care if she ever saw a classroom. All the notes and phone calls that came from the teachers were about Ruby. Ruby didn't do her homework, Ruby came to school with one shoe, Ruby came without a consent form for the outing to the museum, Ruby's failed maths for the fourth time, Ruby's drawings won first prize.

'And you, Ruby? Do you want to go to private school too?'

Ruby licked her fingers. 'I told you, Daddy, I'm going to be an artist.'

'And what kind of money do you think you'll earn?'

'I don't know. But you said we could choose what we want to be when we grow up.'

'Do you want to sell paintings in Greenmarket Square and starve?'

'I'll be married, Daddy. My husband will take care of the money part.'

My father put his fork down, and laughed. When Ruby was three and refused to wear anything but purple underwear, he sent his typist to Woolworths for two dozen in that shade. I had to wait six weeks for Pacman, and Ruby had only to pout and flash those almond eyes and my father would give his okay.

After I'd been at my new school three months, I asked if I could have Jeremy over for the weekend. My mother said yes, but my father couldn't quite wrap himself around the idea of an Afrikaner boy in his home. Family visited on weekends, he said, he didn't want trouble and envy surrounding his son. But he agreed, with conditions and warnings.

The factory closed at four on Fridays, the one day we could count on him to sit down to supper with us, and a favourite time because he would listen to grievances and hand out pocket money, toffee rolls and comic books, putting Milano's troubles behind him for a few hours. I must say I was anxious to see what he thought of my blue-eyed friend – and also a bit nervous about my sisters putting me in the eyes – showing me up. In between helpings of mash and peas, I found him glancing occasionally at Jeremy: how he held the fork, cut his meat, the way he put the food in his mouth – not too different from us except he ate a little slower, giving the food a few more chews. But then Jeremy didn't have three siblings rushing to prong their forks into the last chop. Jeremy had a good way of speaking to his elders, sort of well-behaved without being overly reserved, and my father was impressed by things like that. Of course, he had no idea that Jeremy was the school prankster and Mr Greaves's worst nightmare.

'What're your plans for the future, Jeremy, do you know what you want to be?' I suddenly heard him ask.

'Yes, sir, I want to be a pilot.'

My father's brows rose in surprise. 'That's nice. You like planes then, do you?'

'My father was a fighter pilot.'

'Really?'

'He was killed in an air raid five years ago.'

Something went the wrong way down my father's throat, and he coughed. 'I'm sorry to hear that.'

'That's all right, Mr Samaar. You didn't know.'

'My mom's a designer,' Layla said. 'She makes all the patterns for my father's factory. And yours?'

'She's a police sergeant.'

'A woman police sergeant? Does she come home with a gun?' Ruby asked.

'Don't be silly, Ruby,' Somaya said. 'Sergeants don't carry guns.'

'She does have one,' Jeremy responded. 'I count the bullets sometimes.'

I sat there listening to my sisters ask the questions I hadn't asked, and Jeremy answering all of them. But what a combo for parents. A police sergeant and a fighter pilot, protecting South Africa's inhabitants. Who couldn't be proud of that?

The next morning my father was ready to drive off in his bakkie when Ruby ran out to tell me that Rudwan had just called to say that he would get a lift with his father and would be there soon. I was busy wiping the windscreen, and my father leaned his head out the window. 'He's your cousin, you be nice.' He had this stupid fear that because I was friends with Jeremy, I was going to think I was white. Parents, I tell you. They put you out in this dinghy without a life-jacket, then blame you if you drown.

Rudwan arrived in the middle of our gluing together a complicated windmill made out of sucker sticks, and I knew the minute he pretended Jeremy wasn't in the room that inviting him had been a mistake.

'Let's play kennetjie,' he suggested. He was a whiz at hitting the stubby stick over the roof.

'It's getting dark, and we have to glue everything together tonight. We can't play right now.'

'You can help us,' Jeremy offered.

Rudwan didn't turn his head to acknowledge his presence.

'You forgot how to play kennetjie, now?' he persisted.

'Did I say that? I said it was getting dark. How can we see how to play? And we have to finish this project.'

'Let's do it later,' Jeremy suggested.

'No. Tomorrow it has to be dry.'

Rudwan left mumbling, and moments later my father summoned me into the living room.

'What's going on?'

'He's being stupid.'

'Now he's calling me stupid,' Rudwan whined. 'He's oorgetrek with his friend.'

'I'm not impressed by anyone, you idiot. We have to finish gluing this thing tonight so we can paint it in the morning, and he doesn't understand. He wants to go play kennetjie in the dark.'

'You two always get along; why're you acting this way?'

'He's forgetting who he is.'

It was just the sort of thing to set my father off. I wanted to punch the sneer off Rudwan's face.

'Then why did I ask you to come? And what's the big deal, anyway? We can play tomorrow, and then you can show off!'

'That's it,' Rudwan snorted. 'I'm calling my father to pick me up.'

'Stop this nonsense now,' my father raised his voice. 'You're not calling anyone and, you, mister, I told you beforehand what's what.'

'Are you satisfied now, you snot? We asked if you wanted to help, but you didn't want to. What's your problem, man?'

'Who cares about your stupid project anyway.'

'That's enough!' my father roared. 'Go sort yourselves out, or I'm driving everyone home!'

We slunk back into my room, and I cursed myself for inviting him. Jeremy pretended nothing was wrong, and I felt shitty having him there. We were showing a very bad side. Worse, when I'd told Rudwan he could come, I'd not thought of the sleeping arrangements. To prevent war, I threw three cushions between the twin beds and tossed restlessly all night on the floor, listening to their machine-gun farts.

The next morning, on my way to the bathroom, I overheard my parents in the kitchen. They were up early for koeksisters and coffee.

'... on his best behaviour.'

'So are we.'

'Do you think he's sincere?'

'What do you mean?'

'You can't change what's in their hearts – what they believe.'

'He's just a child.'

'But conditioned from the time he saw his black nanny staring down at him.'

'It's not his fault. And he has no problem having a Muslim boy for a friend. It's today's children who're going to change things, not us.'

'Today's black children, and coloured children. Not them. Do you think that after three centuries, they can flush it out with Epsom salts?'

'You must stop all this politics in front of the kids.'

'They should be aware.'

'What, every kid in South Africa isn't aware?'

There was silence for a moment, then I heard my mother's voice change. 'I still like him, though.'

'Me too.'

'When he said that his father had died in an air raid it kind of did something to me. There is glory in protecting your country.'

1977 had started with black schools reopening amid continued student boycotts, ending with Rhodesia announcing its acceptance of one man, one vote, and black majority rule – a dream held by most but not all of us. Somaya came third in class with 80 per cent, Layla passed with above-average marks, Ruby played the lead in The Frog Prince, I finished a good first year at the new school, and my mother stunned us with the announcement that the Philippi air had thrown her cycle out, and a baby was on the way.

The factory closed for the Christmas holidays, and my father made plans for a trip to the Wilderness. A few days into the arrangements I asked if I could bring Jeremy with.

'You know, Nazeem,' he started, with that resigned thing in his voice, 'I like Jeremy, but he's come here all year now, and he's never asked you to his house.'

'Maybe he has a reason.'

My father looked at me in that strange way. 'Of course he has.'

'He's not like that, Daddy; you don't know him. And we can't blame him for the government.'

'Who said anything about the government? It's you I'm thinking about. Doesn't it bother you that he hasn't asked you once to come and meet his family?'

'It does, when I think about it. I don't know where he lives, and he knows where we keep the cheese in the fridge. I think about it, but I put it out of my mind. We're friends, that hasn't changed, and he's going nowhere for the holidays.'

'His family's never tried to find out about us. I find that very strange also. You don't think we'd let you spend weekends at someone's house without knowing where it is or who those people are? This is two weeks in the Wilderness.'

'His mother's a sergeant, maybe she checked us out.'

My father said no more. That night at supper he brought it up with my mother.

'Bring him with,' she said.

'I don't know why I bother to ask you. You'll bring the whole soccer team if you can. You have four children, you know, not yet five. Don't you find it strange that his mother's never called us, or tried to find out who we are?'

'I do, but if that's how they do things, and Jeremy wants to come, why not?'

The day before the trip my mother and I went to pick Jeremy up. He had given me the address, and I was looking forward to seeing where he lived. I don't know what I expected at 63 Crosby Street, but my spirits sank when we stopped in front of a crumbly-

walled cottage with an overgrown path and a rusted bicycle leaning against a wheelbarrow growing weeds under a mulberry tree,
with trampled berries on the hard ground. I wanted to believe that
we were at the wrong house but then the front door opened and
Jeremy, who must've been watching from the window, came out
with his rucksack and fishing rod. He didn't close the door behind
him, and no one came out to see him off.

Jeremy got into the car, and we all sat heavy with our thoughts.
When we arrived at the wrought-iron gates to Faan and the gar-
deners, with the Dobermans jumping the car, our spirits lifted, and
I was even glad to see my sisters, anxious to show off the trailer my
father had rented.

Later that evening Jeremy and I packed the coolers with frozen
chops and boerewors, afterwards stealing smokes from the head
gardener in the backyard. One of our favourite things was sitting
with Faan and Piet outside their quarters, dragging on their hand-
rolled cigarettes, but that night Jeremy was strangely reserved. I
don't know if it was the tobacco, the coming trip, or picking him
up at his house, but several times while I was chewing the fat with
the boys, I caught him staring off into the dark.

At eleven my mother turned off the TV, and we went to bed.
Shortly after midnight, somewhere in the dimness of sleep, I heard
the gates roll open and the car drive into the garage, and heard
voices. I pricked up my ears, and turned to Jeremy in the next bed.
He wasn't there. Through the window I saw his white hair
reflected in the moonlight, standing on the veranda in the dark.

'… I was waiting to talk to you, Mr Levy.'

'Is something wrong, Jeremy?'

'I just wanted to say that I appreciate it, sir, that you said I could
come along with you. And that I … lied to you that first night.'

'The first night?'

'When I first had supper at your house ten months ago. My father *was* a fighter pilot, and he did die in an air raid – that was the truth. But my mother's not who I said she was.'

'What do you mean?'

'She's a Carnegie from Simonstown. That's what I've been told. She gave me up when I was born.'

'I see.'

'Elspeth is the woman who looks after me. She and my father never married, but I look on her as my mother. Elspeth's a cashier at OK Bazaars.'

'Jeremy, I — '

'When my father died, Elspeth moved to Woodstock, and took me with her. Her boyfriend lives with us.'

'Do you have any other relatives, Jeremy?'

'An auntie in Jo'burg. She sends me a card at Christmas time. I haven't seen her since I was eight.'

I sank back into my pillow, with the same hollow feeling as the time Miss Thebus in Standard Three had told us that Merle, the girl who sat next to me in class, had died of TB.

I watched them there in the moonlight, my oppositionist father and my silver-haired friend.

'Do you think, Jeremy, that these figs will be ripe by the time we get back from the trip? My wife planted this tree five years ago, and every year these small little things come out and drop rock-hard to the ground.'

Of course, we never spoke about it, Jeremy and me. On the trip my heart swelled when I saw my mother drape his socks over a branch to dry, and my father include him in everything. I turned the chops on the braai, noticing my parents for the first time. Maybe one day one of them or Jeremy will tell me about it and I won't have to wade through all the Carnegies in the phone book.

Billie can't poo

In a small town like Peterborough in the early seventies, you didn't meet many South Africans. But suddenly there she was at the desk Mr Chapman's secretary used to occupy, plugged into the dictaphone, looking over a file. 'Bitchy,' some of the girls said, avoiding her in the lunch room. 'Judgemental and uptight.'

They were right. Everything that came out of her mouth was a biting remark. Canadians were insipid, ungrateful, unappreciative. They had to live in a country where you stood in the rain for a bus while an empty one for whites went by, to understand the freedom they had.

The office played in a bowling league, and Sabah and her husband, Miles, were on our team. There wasn't much chatter those first months – Sabah throwing mostly gutter balls, not good at any sports, she claimed. Still, we did somehow become friends, hard and fast by the end of the season when she threw a bad ball, costing us the game, and Miles had shown his true colours. She spoke of her marriage. The problem wasn't infidelity, cheating or physical abuse, but a lie six years ago when he'd promised her that they would move to South Africa if she married him. In the end, after two children, he just laughed and said Canada was where his mother was.

I didn't know Ella from Lena before meeting Sabah, but took to going to her house on the weekends to listen to her great collection of jazz and stories of home. She'd grown up with the sounds of Satchmo, Gillespie and the Monk, she said – both her brothers were sax players. One Saturday I arrived to a van outside the house, and Miles packing all his belongings into it. When the van had disappeared down the road, she turned to me. 'I'm going home to catch my breath for a few weeks, Billie. Wanna come?'

When the plane descended over DF Malan Airport in Cape Town, she burst out crying.

'Sabah, what's the matter?'

She pointed to the mountains below. I had seen these mountains in postcards, and heard much about them from her, but nothing prepared me for their size and dominance over the city.

'I don't cry when I leave, Billie. I cry when I come.'

It was a first for me, seeing her vulnerable like this.

At least 50 people were at the airport to meet us, with bags and parcels and flowers and a guava juice someone had popped into my hand, everyone talking at once.

The first problem, scarcely ten minutes on South African soil, was who had first rights to us. Mrs Dollie – she'd gone back to her maiden name – claimed that as she was the mother, she deserved the honour of Sabah coming home to her house, so the destination was Athlone, and 'Please, everybody, we'll see you there.' Mr Solomon, Sabah's father, said that he had specially prepared a room with two single beds for Sabah and her friend, that his ex-wife didn't have first rights and that Sabah was going with him to Walmer Estate. Sabah's eldest brother, Riaz, then chimed in, saying he was married now, had a big house, and wanted his sister with him. All this in the parking lot while cousins and uncles and aunts waited to hear in which direction they should point their cars. In the end, Sabah refused to go anywhere and they finally agreed to one day with her mother, one day with her father, and weekends left open for brothers, cousins and friends.

I stood with my bags at my feet listening. This wasn't the city I'd imagined and heard so much about. I'd expected unrest, a darkness of spirit. Cape Town was nothing like that. The day was hot, sunny and bright – a far cry from the grey skies of Peterborough – Table Mountain beckoning. And all around me were the sounds of the family, all speaking as fast as Sabah. I knew I was in for a heck of a holiday.

Mrs Dollie's house was a lovely, whitewashed, Spanish-style bungalow, chockful with antiques, African rugs and artefacts, with a pool surrounded by some unusual thorn and red-leaved trees in the yard. Mrs Dollie couldn't swim, and had once fallen into the pool trying to manoeuvre an avocado from a branch overhead. Two people had to get her out, even though the water was only six feet deep.

'Don't stand near the edge, Billie,' she warned. 'They wait for you to stand there in your nice clothes, then chuck you in. Riaz is just a terrible boy. When this house was first built and the Imam came to bless it, he knocked the Imam into the pool, clothes and all.'

Riaz laughed.

'Don't laugh,' Mrs Dollie said. 'The poor man's fez was floating in the deep end, he almost drowned.'

'Serves him right for telling us Muslims shouldn't have pools.'

Mrs Dollie lived alone with her youngest son, Fa'iq, and there was ample room, she said, so she didn't know why Sabah still had to go and sleep at her father's as if he deserved equal time. The kitchen was noisy with aunts and neighbours pouring tea, all waiting to hear about Canada. Mrs Dollie clucked like an excited hen over the proceedings.

That first night, watching Sabah with her family, the bossa nova rhythms of Stan Getz swelling and dipping over the laughter and noise, and tea and coffee coming non-stop from the kitchen with plates of jam tarts, custard rolls and chocolate éclairs, I felt swept up by the wave of events. No one was concerned about how much they ate, or the order in which food was served, and I watched enviously as brothers and cousins and friends just dug into dessert, later rounding it all off with chicken breyani and mango juice. Where I came from, you had to be invited to a meal. You said grace, you started with salad or soup, and everyone sat down, all at the same time. If there was music, it was usually some classical piece my father put on to aid digestion. The meal was understated, and you ate just enough. There was dessert only on weekends, and it would be nothing more than custard with canned fruit, or a slice of fruitcake.

'You know, I've never heard a girl swear like that,' a striking man in a cream suit, who had sat quietly all evening, suddenly said.

'Really?' Sabah responded. 'And who're you?'

'Your future brother-in-law, Suleiman Adams. My sister, Toeghfa over there, is engaged to your brother, Fa'iq.'

'She's a doctor,' Mrs Dollie said proudly. 'From the Bo-Kaap. Fa'iq, didn't you introduce Toeghfa to Sabah?'

'Have I had a chance to say anything with you talking, Ma?' Fa'iq laughed. 'Yes, I did introduce Toeghfa.'

Suleiman continued with Sabah, obviously fascinated by her. 'I've never heard the f-word used with so many variations,' he said. He turned to Sabah's mother in wonderment. 'I didn't know, Mrs Dollie, that you have a daughter like this.'

Mrs Dollie laughed as if someone had praised her. 'She's like that. She's very naughty.' She made no move to say anything to

Sabah. Sabah could've done a somersault on the oak table, she would've loved it. She was just too glad for her daughter to be there. I became aware of myself as I sat there grinning, the onlooker, the friend. I was in an environment entirely different from my own in Canada. My home was a quiet one, with my mother playing bridge with friends on Tuesday nights, and my father building model airplanes in the basement in his spare time. A party would consist of no more than six or eight people in the backyard having a barbecue and one or two beers. It was in Cape Town that I really came to see who Sabah was.

Suleiman came to the Dollie house several times, taking us out for scenic drives and dinners, trying to gain Sabah's interest. But Sabah was only at the beginning of her grief over her broken marriage, and wasn't interested in anyone. That didn't mean, though, that she didn't have a darn good time teasing the heck out of Suleiman.

When the last guests finally left at around two in the morning, and I was starting to feel dizzy from the long flight and all the excitement, Sabah said she was taking a quick drive in her mother's car to Sea Point. She always went to this one particular place on her first night home. So off we went, in the middle of the night, up the mountainous De Waal Drive, overlooking the city and harbour lights, comforted by the smoothness of the Citroën on the winding road. Fifteen minutes later we arrived on Beach Road to the crashing sea and the rich salt air filling the car.

Driving past apartment blocks and restaurants, we came to a lonely spot along the promenade with a bench. She stopped. The bench was wet, and in front of it was a railing. Below the railing the waves rolled thunderously over the rocks, and splashed with great force over our heads, hitting the pavement. I saw a huge spray of foam rise up and quickly ran back to the car.

'This is it, Billie! This is it!' she thrilled, holding on to the railing, turning her nose to the sky as the sea smacked into her. The girl was mad, I thought, as I watched through the car window. She was revelling in it. Finally, she got back into the car with sopping jeans. We drove back without a word. That was Sabah. High, with long moments of silence. I had seen this, even in Canada. She would invite me over for supper after work. We would have a grand time playing Scrabble with her children – both her children were already avid players at the ages of eight and ten – and she would talk about her life back home, and then for no reason, she would fall silent. I never asked what she was thinking about. I knew. Her longing to return to South Africa for good was far more sorrowful than her disintegrating marriage. 'A man I can get anywhere, Billie. I'm not saying he can replace the father. But a man I can find anywhere. I can't find me a new family.'

Hardly six hours later the telephone rang. It was Sabah's father asking what time we were coming. He was planning a braai for his side of the family, and expected us no later than two. Fa'iq drove us to Walmer Estate, where the house and yard were crowded with people excited to see Sabah, Riaz standing in shorts in front of a smoking brick barbecue turning sausages and chops. The noise was deafening. Mr Solomon had four Dobermans – his 'built-in alarm system', he said – and the Solomon men were such a loud bunch you could hear them all the way down at the store. Once, the story went – while listening to a boxing match on the kitchen radio in the sixties, the dogs panting at their feet – they were making such a racket cheering on the great Cassius Clay that burglars had come in through the bedroom window and stolen all the blankets from the beds.

Bright and early the morning following the braai, Mrs Dollie telephoned Sabah's father's house, saying she missed us and that Sabah had been at her father's long enough. And so it went, with phone calls back and forth every morning from one house to the other.

When we'd been in Cape Town three days and I still hadn't gone to the bathroom, I felt a little less strange and asked Mrs Dollie if she had a laxative. She gave me a dose of castor oil, squeezing the juice of an orange onto my tongue afterwards. 'Best thing, Billie,' she said. 'I always gave Sabah and her brothers this when they were small. It'll work. Probably you're a little constipated because this is all so strange to you. It can upset your routine.'

Riaz and his wife, Saliyah, came over for breakfast that morning.

'And how're the Canadians?' Riaz asked.

'Billie can't poo,' Mrs Dollie said.

'Billie can't poo? What do you mean, Billie can't poo? Billie, can't you poo?'

I didn't know where to put my face.

'Did you go since you came?' he asked, forking a grilled kidney into his mouth.

'No.'

'Billie's sitting vas,' Mrs Dollie said.

'What's that?' I asked.

'My mother said you sat it into a cement block on the plane.'

Everyone laughed.

'What's the matter with you guys?' Sabah said. 'Leave Billie alone.'

'What did you give her, Mom?' Riaz asked.

'Castor oil.'

'Castor oil? Billie needs a bomb, not castor oil. I'll go to the chemist and get her something.'

'Wait till tomorrow,' Mrs Dollie said. 'I gave her two teaspoons.

We don't want Billie having accidents in her pants. Aren't you going to Caledon with Toyer tomorrow?'

'The day after. We're going to Daddy's this afternoon.'

'I don't see why your father should get so many turns.'

'We'll give you a lift,' Riaz said.

'Listen, don't you be in a hurry to take them away. I gave them the other car. Your father can wait his turn.'

'You gave them the Volksie, Ma? That car's dangerous.'

'They're not getting the Citroën again. You should see what they did to the seats, it was soaking wet. If they don't like the Volksie, Fa'iq can take them when he gets up. And he's another one. He came in at four this morning.'

'My mother's nagging, Billie, because Fa'iq's getting married in June. She misses him already.'

'He can be gone now, Billie, for all I care. Leaving his clothes on the bathroom floor and never making up his bed. And I have to beg him to put the chemicals in the pool or to vacuum it. I won't take his side one bit if Toeghfa complains. Fa'iq!' she shouted towards the back of the house. 'Breakfast!'

'She's a pretender,' Riaz said. 'Fa'iq's her favourite. Tell her, Ma, how you always brag that he's the only one who remembers Mother's Day. My mother's such a patsy for a phone call and chocolates, even if he takes the twenty right out of her purse to buy it.'

We arrived at the house on the hill late in the afternoon. Mr Solomon was drinking tea with two men on the stoep, playing dominoes.

'Billie! Where were you yesterday? Did you go out? We were waiting for you to play cards.' I'd become a favourite, and taught them how to play scat.

'We went to town with Fa'iq.'

'And Friday we're going with Toyer to Caledon,' Sabah added.

'Billie wants to go to a spa. Toyer also needs a woman to help in the house. He wants to get one from the farm.'

'What're you going with Toyer for? He's no relative of yours. Now everyone wants a piece of your time. You're only here for a month.'

'Don't be selfish, Daddy. We're all going. Fa'iq, Toeghfa, maybe even Suleiman.'

'That drip?'

'You're just jealous because none of your children are doctors.'

'Billie, have you seen that boy? He sits so upright, you can boil an egg in his bum.'

'Mr Solomon!' I have to say that I liked him. I liked the whole family, but he and his ex-wife were at the top of my list.

'That's right, Billie. All that studying's turned him into a prune. Even I have a better sense of humour than that *doos*. So, what do you think of our beautiful country, Billie? Tell Mr Lawrence and Mr Fish what you think.'

'Well, Mr Solomon, I didn't see anyone with beads and feathers running around in the streets. Where're the Zulus?'

He had an infectious laugh. 'So that's what the Canadians think of us?'

'Billie has a problem,' Riaz said.

'What's the problem?'

'Billie can't poo.'

'Billie can't poo? My goodness, nasty. Why can't you poo, Billie?'

'I don't know,' I said, hoping for cramps.

'When was the last time you went to the toilet?'

'In Canada,' Riaz laughed.

'Canada! Billie, you can poison yourself. You have a nerve to come and contaminate our land.'

I tell you my face was red most days in his company. He was the most outspoken man I'd ever met. I could see where Sabah got her attitude from. Her tenacity she got from her mother, but the spirit was all Solomon.

'Don't make fun of my friend,' Sabah said, 'She already had castor oil.'

'My wife has some brown pills,' Mr Fish said. 'I can pop over to the house later on and get some. Mr Solomon knows she always had that problem with open bowels.'

Mr Lawrence chimed in. 'Eat lots of pineapple, that's the best thing. All that acid will bring anything down. Don't they have pineapples in Canada?'

'Of course they have pineapples in Canada. How can Mr Lawrence then ask such a stupid question?' Mr Solomon asked.

'Ag, their pineapples are not like ours. Listen to me – what's your name? Billie? Listen to me, Billie. Forget all these remedies. Just eat pineapple tonight. No meat and rice. And pineapple again in the morning. I guarantee you'll go.'

'Does Mr Lawrence then want her to turn into a pineapple? Look at her, she already looks a little yellow around the gills.'

They burst out laughing, Mr Solomon leading the pack.

'Don't worry, Billie, I have a good remedy for open bowels. I've got something in the kitchen that's bound to work. I made it four days ago.'

'And if Mr Solomon's ginger beer doesn't move you,' Mr Lawrence said, 'nothing will.'

'That's right, Billie. Then we might as well take you in the van to Groote Schuur.'

And they burst out laughing all over again.

'I told you,' Sabah said to me. 'My family's not well. My father can go on like this forever. He loves it.'

'Come, Billie, let's go inside. What kind of a name is Billie, anyway? The name Billie in this country always comes with a pair of horns.'

'You're too much, Mr Solomon.' I felt a genuine affection for him.

I noted the difference in the two households. At the Dollie house, everything was spotless and in its place, with fresh flowers and lovely aromas. The radio was on low, the music switched off at sunset for half an hour to respect the maghrib prayers. You ate on time and you prayed on time. The Solomon place, on the other hand, was like a beach house for teenagers. There were sand prints from Dobermans, dirty ashtrays, dog bowls, piles of old newspapers and packs of cards right next to the condensed milk and sugar on the kitchen counter. The music was never switched off, and the fridge, when I opened it to get a can of condensed milk for Mr Solomon's tea, made me take a step back. Nothing was sealed, and a big pot was jammed in on the same shelf with an opened can of peas, an overripe tomato, four biscuits on a saucer, and a half-eaten egg sandwich on a plate.

When we had been in Cape Town just a week, a relative died. After the funeral, ten of us were back around the huge table in the Solomon kitchen feeling depressed, and someone suggested gin rummy to cheer us up.

'No,' Sabah said. 'We have to have respect. How can we play cards when someone just died? The man's hardly cold.'

'Ag, what,' Mr Solomon said, 'Boeta Braim would *want* us to enjoy ourselves. Riaz, get the cards. Toeghfa, put on the kettle for tea, my girl. Let's have a few hands for Boeta Braim.'

That's how it was. I liked being in his house. There were no rules, no formal times for eating, and until you got hungry, no one knew whether someone was going to throw a few onions and potatoes and meat in a pot, or whether you were going to get a steak salad sandwich from Wembley. The spontaneity was completely in keeping with his character – which was also the same for Sabah.

Mr Solomon and I went into the oak-trim kitchen. Everything in there he'd built with his own hands, he said, and showed me the missing thumb to prove it. He led me to two huge paraffin tins on the floor. He lifted the lid and the pungent ginger aroma hit my nose.

Riaz put out eight glasses. Mr Solomon took a mug, dipped it into the fizzing brew, and poured the potent brown liquid into a glass, giving Sabah a first taste.

'Whooofff!' she said, blinking her eyes. 'This kicks!'

I took a sip and felt the fire rip down my throat.

'What did I tell you, hey?' he smiled proudly. 'No later than tomorrow, Billie, you'll sing the national anthem.'

I couldn't wait. Anyone's national anthem. Even God Save the Queen. But nothing happened, and we spent the next morning playing cards in our pyjamas and gowns with friends who had come to find out which horses Mr Solomon was favouring for the jackpot, Mr Solomon all the while continuing to pour ginger beer into my glass. At lunch time there was the horn of a car hooting impatiently outside – Mrs Dollie in her polished Citroën, waiting to take us to Wynberg.

Mr Solomon raised his right brow in that way he had when he was about to get cocky. 'Your mother's getting mighty bold driving that car up my street every day,' he said to no one in particular. 'I wouldn't be surprised if that woman still has a thing for me. Ever since I saw her in Salt River a few weeks ago, she's getting brave. I tell you, Billie, she couldn't get out of that car fast enough, preening like a peacock, almost falling over her feet.'

'Oh, stop it, Daddy,' Sabah said. 'You think everyone's in love with you.'

We said goodbye and jumped into the car, pyjamas and all, and then had to listen to Mrs Dollie's version of how she had bumped into the old goat in Salt River, and he purposely parking his van behind her to have a better look. The man had to get over his ridiculousness. He was almost sixty.

It was a scorching day. We decided to spend the afternoon playing Scrabble by the pool.

'It's a heatwave out there,' Mrs Dollie shouted from the kitchen window. 'I'm not coming out. You girls can come in if you want something to drink.'

'I'm taking off my bather, Billie,' Sabah said, pulling the straps off her shoulder, stepping out of it, jumping into the pool. I sat for a few minutes watching her head break the surface, then her bum as she dived down again.

Her mother, despite what she'd said, came out with tall glasses of chilled guava juice on a tray.

'Mom, you have to keep watch,' Sabah said from the pool. 'I'm skinny-dipping.'

'Skinny-dipping? What nonsense is this? Is that what you learned in Canada? To swim without clothes on? If my mother was alive now, she'd die all over again.'

'Don't be such a prude, Mom, it's just us. Who's here to see?'

'God sees.' She pretended to be cross, and went back inside, nodding her head.

Sabah got out of the pool. 'Ever pee standing up, Billie?'

'What?'

She walked around the pool to the grass on the other side. 'You stand like this, and you lean your leg slightly inwards, then you let the pee run down your thigh.' She closed her eyes to the sun, smiling like the devil as the pee trailed down her leg into the grass.

'God, this feels good! It's such a nice warm feeling against your leg. And straight into the ground. Don't you have to pee?'

Swimming without bathing suits, peeing on your own foot? Was this the frigid bitch everyone at the office had said had a peg up her arse?

Then we saw Suleiman Adams come through the garage. Mrs Dollie must've been performing her prayers and not heard him knock. I looked at Sabah. She had also just registered his presence and become aware of her nakedness. But she didn't jump back into the pool. She looked at him, smiling innocently.

'You're naked,' he said.

'Well, yeah. Wait till my mother sees you.'

I rolled up her towel and tossed it over. It was a foot or so short of landing on the other side and she could've caught it, but she let it fall into the pool.

'Maybe I should go back out again,' he said.

'Throw my bather, Billie.'

This she caught, and stepped into, wriggling into the wet suit as Suleiman tried hard to keep his eyes on the trees.

'That's a nice bather,' he smiled when she walked past him.

'Not nice buns?'

'That too. Are you married?'

'Almost not.'

'What does that mean?'

'It means that I am, and that soon I won't be.'

We left early the next morning for Caledon, six of us jammed into Toyer's hump-backed Volvo. My stomach had rumbled a few times, giving me hope, and I was a little uncomfortable sitting between Sabah and Toeghfa in the back.

We stopped along the side of the road just before going on to

Sir Lowry's Pass. Toeghfa took out a hamper from the trunk.

'Salmon sandwiches, anyone? Mince pies?'

'Toeghfa makes good sandwiches,' Fa'iq said.

'I'm having some really bad cramps,' I told Sabah.

'Do you have to go?'

'I don't know. It's all in my stomach still.'

'You can't pick a worse place than this, Billie. We're right in the open. We'll have to drive quite a distance when we cross the pass before we find any trees.'

The cramps subsided a bit, and I had coffee and sandwiches with them.

Riaz took out a joint. 'Skuif, Billie?'

'Wait till your wife hears about this,' Sabah said, taking a few heavy drags. She exhaled, giving a naughty smile. 'We don't have this quality in Canada.'

We all stood around trekking skuif – I was picking up the lingo – and I almost forgot about the cramps.

We got back in the car and headed up the pass.

Two minutes later the cramps were back, and moved with knife-like force into my bowels.

'Can you stop the car?'

'What is it, Billie?' Sabah asked.

'It's an emergency. Please!'

'Oh, my word,' Toyer said. 'We can't stop here, we're climbing. Can you hold it in?'

'No.' I was close to panic.

We were in a line of cars high up on the mountain. When I looked down at the steep fall, I got dizzy. We moved higher, around a dangerous curve.

'Please, stop, I have to get out!'

Toyer put on the indicator and came to an abrupt halt. I climbed hastily over Toeghfa, who was taking too long to get out. Out on the narrow gravel shoulder, I ripped at my jeans. I didn't dare look over the cliff and didn't care about the cars coming up the hill or the wind blowing up my arse. I hit everything, including the tyre of the car.

'Holy, fuck!' Sabah exclaimed, 'she's right next to the car. Give me something to cover her up.'

'There's a blanket in the back.'

Sabah got out and opened the trunk, and took out an old picnic blanket. She held the blanket in front of me as a shield while I squatted and did my business – on and on, three minutes, six minutes, ignoring the bypassers or those in the car politely busying themselves.

'Look at these fuckers staring. What're you looking at?' she snarled at an old couple in a white Toyota Cressida.

'I'm sorry, Sabah. I'm so ashamed. Do you have any tissues?'

'Toeghfa,' she thumped on the window. 'Some napkins, please.'

'Napkins?'

'Serviettes!'

'We used them when we had the sandwiches.'

I was in a strange country with my arse over a cliff, shitting all over my jeans. Who would believe such a story? And who would've just packed up and crossed continents anyway with a co-worker they hardly knew?

'Isn't there any paper in the car?' she asked again.

'Only Riaz's Times. Do you want that?'

'I haven't looked at it yet,' Riaz said.

'Don't get kak now, Riaz,' Sabah hissed. 'Hand it over.'

'I'll give you the property guide. I don't read that. Or do you want the sports section?'

'Just any flippin' section! You want Billie to die out here?'

She handed me some of the paper.

'What about my jeans? I can't keep them on. O my God, this is so embarrassing.'

She tore off more paper and handed it to me. 'Billie, it's just us here. Take off your jeans. You'll have to sit in this blanket.'

I stepped out of my pants, and with my foot scraped both my jeans and my mess over the cliff. Then kicked over my shoes. My bum burned. I felt crampy and soiled.

'Is there any water?' I asked.

'Some water here, please,' Sabah said.

Toeghfa handed her a bottle, which she gave to me. I washed my hands and my feet. Wrapped like a mummy from the waist down, I got back into the car.

'My father and his bladdy ginger beer,' Riaz said. 'You okay, Billie?'

'I'm fine, thanks.'

'Wat nou, mense?' Toyer asked. 'What now, people?'

'Draai om,' Riaz said. 'Turn around. We can't go with Billie in a blanket to a spa.'

When Mr Solomon heard what had happened, he gloated all over again about the potency of his home brew. For days there were enquiries about my bowels, and advice on follow-up maintenance. Mr Lawrence brought a box of pineapples and a few packets of dried fruit, just in case, and even Suleiman brought prunes.

There was only one incident during my visit to Cape Town to really remind me where I was. Sabah and I had to go to pick up something for her mother at a shop in Athlone and returned to find the car standing on four bricks. We couldn't believe it. The tyres had been stolen in broad daylight right in front of the Athlone Police Station.

The constable on duty had a friendly smile, and pointed us to the other side of the wooden partition.

'I want to report a theft,' Sabah said.

'Over there, miss,' he said again. 'You're standing in the section for non-whites.'

'I'm not white.'

'Please,' he smiled patiently, 'if you go over there, someone can take your complaint.'

'I don't want to go over there.'

'Where do you live?' he asked.

'I don't live in this country. My mother lives in Athlone. Now, can I tell you what I'm here for? Our car was parked outside, and — '

'Miss, look, I'm sorry. If you and your friend – and don't tell me she's from Athlone too – if the two of you want to go over there, Constable Van Rijn can look after you.'

'Can you believe this, Billie? They can't make up their minds what the fuck I am. First I'm not white enough, and now I'm not black enough!'

I didn't know what she was talking about. She refused to do what the cop asked, and we went back outside. In the end we went looking for a public telephone to call Fa'iq to come and sort it all out.

A few days before our departure I noticed that Mrs Dollie was no longer clamouring for Sabah's attention. In fact, she seemed to be attempting to create some distance. Coming into the kitchen early one morning, I caught her deep in thought at the sink, looking through the window at the trees in the yard. Sabah had warned me. Her mother went into mourning while she was still there.

'And what are your plans for today, Mrs Dollie?'

'Oh, nothing,' she said, not her usual perky self. 'I think I'll stay home and make some pastries for next week. Are you missing Canada?'

'I miss my mother, yes.'

'What's a mother, hey? All children are the same. My own mother died six months after Sabah left in 1968. I still miss her today. Can you believe that? A grown woman like me. Sometimes, when I think of Sabah so far away, I cry for my mother, and I cry for Sabah. My mother always used to say that you can have ten sons, it doesn't equal one girl. My sons are good sons, Billie, don't get me wrong. But sons are not like daughters. They take wives and move on with their lives. A daughter is yours, no matter who she's with. Do you have any brothers?'

'I'm an only child.'

'Shame. That must be lonely for you.'

'I'm used to it, Mrs Dollie. My mother and I are friends. We play bridge together in a club.'

'That's nice. Me and Sabah are close, too. We did a lot of things together before she left for Canada. Did she tell you why she went?'

'No.'

She was silent for a while, then looked up at me. 'Maybe one day she will.'

In Walmer Estate, Mr Solomon also was saying his own goodbyes.

'I'm not coming to the airport on Friday,' he mumbled one night when we went to see him. There were no cards, no visitors. The evening paper lay folded on the chair in the front room.

'It's all right,' Sabah said.

'And don't still come out of your way to drive here when you leave. I'll say goodbye to you on the phone.'

'Okay, Daddy.'

Then his expression changed, and he seemed almost cross. 'I don't know when you're coming home, Sabah. You've been there eight years now.'

Sabah came to sit next to him. 'We've been through this before, Daddy. I have children there.'

'We all have children.'

'I know. But my children's father lives in Canada. He won't come here, and I can't take them away from him.'

Nothing more was said.

On the day of our departure, Sabah asked Riaz to take her first to her father's house before heading for the airport. She'd tried all day to get him on the telephone. When we got to the Solomon house, there was no one there. Which in itself was very unusual, as Mr Solomon never liked to leave the house, even to go shopping. Mr Lawrence or one of his sons had to pick up things for him.

Our bags were checked in, and we started to edge towards the metal gate. All around us, sad faces looked on, people pushing chocolates and gifts into our hands. I noticed a hardness in Sabah. There was no emotion. Her mother was crying into a wad of tissues, supported by Toeghfa and Saliya on the bench.

'All right, Mom,' she said, getting ready to go through the security gate. 'Till next time, hey?'

Mrs Dollie blew harder into her tissues.

'Don't let me leave like this, Mom.'

'Go, Sabah,' Fa'iq pushed her off. 'Leave Mummy with us.'

'Look after her, Saliya. You too, Toeghfa.'

We stepped through the metal gate. On the plane we said a few words to each other, and she went to sleep. She was that other Sabah again. Somewhere over Africa, I started to feel weepy.

'What's wrong, Billie? Why are you crying?' She had woken up.

'I don't know. I just feel strange.'

She summoned the stewardess, who took me to the crew's quarters, where I was given a tranquilliser.

When I look back on that trip, I can't say what happened. If it was the sea air, the magic of Africa, or the level of intimacy I experienced with Sabah's family. I just know that I sat on that plane, and felt very exhausted. And alone.

'They robbed me, Billie,' was all she said when we touched down on the icy runway at Toronto. 'They robbed me, those fucking bastards.'

Give them too much

Cheeky, these coloureds are getting, I tell you. Some of them downright cocky since they took down the signs and Clifton looking like wild rice on mash – mealies and blankets and children with soggy diapers right next to where your neighbour's stirring his drink. They don't know how to behave now that they're allowed on our beaches. Give them your finger, and you have an epidemic on your hands.

I do the books at Rolaine's, behind where the designers have their drawing boards, and Mr David sometimes gets his hand snagged in a model's underpants. There're benefits, of course, keeping still and saying nothing while his hand crawls up your thigh like the Nile into Egypt in search of its wet beginnings – discounts in the showroom, a raise, the opportunity to go on a trip to Europe – and most girls just fear for their jobs.

The directors of the company are notorious for their antics, Mr David not alone in his harassment of coloured girls. His brother, Mr Saul, at least offers biscuits first before nailing a model or a designer behind the door. The darky from the Malay Quarter who'd cried wolf when Mr Saul slipped his hand down her blouse, and was then told that her shorthand sucked and got sacked, was the one to shake them up. Her father appeared at the factory with

records from Woodstock Typing School, threatening sexual harassment in a climate where breast brushings and lascivious come-ons
were commonplace, and no one gave a damn. Shocked by the con-
frontation, however, the brothers offered her back her job. She
quit, and had a lawyer's letter sent, managing to temper Mr Saul's
behaviour for a few months. Cheeky, I said. Next thing you know,
they'll think you want them sitting next to you on the train.

I've been with Rolaine's 30 years, and seen all the goings-on.
The brothers are known for their swollen glands. When girls with
tuppence to their names accompany Heidi, the head designer, to
Paris for fashion shows, I know one of them's played hide-the-
salami. I pay the medical accounts, and see the unlisted procedures
no one can explain. Do they think I was born yesterday? And do
they think their wives don't know? The wives have their own spies
in the factory, and even know the names of the girls. But it's easier
to pretend not to know. The wives come in on Fridays with their
red lips and beehives just to show they're still on the throne, then
return to their pedicures and charities, and lunch at the President.
I've been a target myself when my tits were under my chin, and my
hair so long, Mr Saul actually tried to grab me in the passage by it
once. But 50's old now for double-breasted dragons with slicked-
down hair lusting after leather bras. And who wants an old tongue
that's been everywhere?

Still, life's not bad if you don't take too seriously all this new
unrest sweeping the country since De Klerk lost his mind. The
man's been too long in the sun. South Africa's managed for 300
years. They couldn't possibly be serious about a black man for a
President. Are they mad?

After depositing my pay on Friday afternoons, I visit Esther
Moen up in Vredehoek, and we sit on the veranda overlooking the
harbour, drinking gin and talking about our children living over-

seas. Her sons in Madrid, my Colin and Glenda in the UK. Children today don't have the same loyalties.

'I'm sorry, Mom,' Glenda had said when she and her husband broke the news that they were emigrating. 'We don't want to raise our children in this environment.'

'But this is your environment. You have everything of the best here.'

At least Glenda writes, and Colin calls every three months. Not Esther's children. Esther's had a rough time. Both boys are homosexuals – 'gays' they call them now. What the hell is gay about one man licking another man's private parts? She had to be glad they were out of her sight, frolicking in Spain. It has to be a helluva jolt discovering a vibrator the size of your arm in your son's chest of drawers.

Poor Esther. Bad things came to her all at once. She used to be a beauty in her day, but when she lost that glow, she also lost her husband to a young waitress. A lot of this seems to be going on. Thank God, my Harry just died of a stroke.

When Esther starts to get maudlin after too much gin and I can't take it, I call Mavis to see if she's free to take in a flick. Mavis and I know each other since high school, and despite what she's done to herself, I still like her company. When her husband ran off five years ago with a girl in a training bra, Mavis had a complete breakdown, and went to Europe for three months. She returned with a new face, hard tits, and a craving for young boys. When I saw that pony-tailed stud with the bulging crotch open the door of her MG in front of Charlie Zee's, I knew Mavis was paying for it.

I am lonesome for a nice gentleman caller, though. A funny thing happens to a woman after 50. There's that terrible stretch looming, and one has to put by, along with the pension fund, a little male companionship just in case. I've no intention ending up walking a poodle alone on the promenade. But then that's the problem being cooped up all day with trial balances in a back room, your only male contacts the driver, a tea boy, cutters and sewing-machine mechanics. And they all come to me with their problems.

'Mrs B,' Mr David said to me the other day, 'I want you to talk to Danny. He's been getting cheeky with those Merriweather people again. I just got a call from the manager.'

'Why don't you lay him off for a week to teach him a lesson?'

'He's got six children, don't be daft. Speak to him.'

And if it isn't Mr David or Mr Saul getting me to sort out their problems, it's the machinists. Do I have a sticker on my forehead saying 'Complaints Bureau'? I don't think so. Although I must say I like being Mother Superior to some of them. When Melvin rolls in the tea trolley, I always ask about his crippled son. I'm not one for snubbing them like that English snot up in the front talking to buyers on the telephone in that phoney accent.

I'm friendly with all of them, particularly the designers. Except for Heidi, who's German, and Pamela, who's white like me, they're all Muslim. Coming from families of tailors and dressmakers, the Muslims have a knack for pattern-making and design. And some of them – now, I'd never say this out loud because if there's one thing you learn in a place like this, it's that a coloured must never be complimented to his face – but some of them, I swear, are more genuine than whites. Except I could never figure out that new one they hired last year.

It wasn't that Hala Baker was rude or impolite, but she had an aloofness about her that grated on me. During tea breaks, while she would offer you a biscuit or sweet from her tin, she never joined in when we talked about the Greenbergs, and wasn't at all like the others trying to ingratiate themselves.

Then that thing happened in the design room one cold after-noon when Mr David came sniffing around, and I was adding up

accounts in the back room, on the other side of a thin partition. I
knew the other designers were out on the floor, Hala the only one
there. I strained my ears, but couldn't hear anything. Just when I
had my fingers poised over the adding machine to continue my
work, there was her voice – 'Mr David, I'm sorry!' – in a tone I'd
never heard before. Seconds later, Mr David, acting like a badly
frightened puppy, came storming out in a snit.

It was obvious what had happened. When the other designers
came back, I had my ear pressed to the wall. But Hala Baker mentioned nothing of the incident to them. I envied her that control –
an arrogance you'll find with a lot of them. They're staunch, I'll
give them that. The worst one will fast during the holy month. But
they have a pride, especially on Fridays when they get two hours
for lunch to attend mosque, and in Ramadan when they're fasting.
They'll sit there with their parched lips and stiff smiles showing
you how your biscuits and tea don't affect them, and you just
know they think they're closer to God. Would God have given this
land to the Christians if they were the chosen ones? Once I made a
batch of apricot tarts for a kitchen tea for one of them and the girl
had the temerity to ask if I'd used lard. As if I didn't know their rule
about bacon and pork.

Not long after this incident with Mr David trying his luck,
Heidi told me that Hala was getting married in Woodstock Town
Hall, and had invited all of them. I hadn't even known she was
engaged. Secretive, I thought. Sweet on top, but probably the kind
that when you lifted up the toaster, you'd find a month's crumbs
underneath.

Muslims, we all know, give fairytale weddings, spending
ridiculous amounts on flower girls, page boys, horse-drawn car-
riages and several costume-changes, and I knew the reception
would be a lavish affair. Marnie had gotten married the previous

year – don't ask me how he managed it on a cutter's wage – and it was an event fit for Ali Baba and all 40 thieves and their wives. I thought longingly of how I'd look in my green silk dress.

But Hala Baker didn't invite me.

'I'm going to the shop, Mrs B,' Melvin came limping in a few minutes before lunch. 'You want anything?'

'Which shop are you going to?'

'Danny's giving me and Miss Heidi a lift to Adderley Street. She's buying the present and the card for everyone to sign. I also have to buy my own present.'

'Your own?'

'A person can't go empty-handed, mos. My wife already bought the doilies.'

'I see. I can't believe Danny's so generous, giving you a lift in his lunch time.'

Melvin laughed, 'That's because he's too lazy to go into the shop himself. And a lousy R5 he gives for a present, troo's Gawd. What kind of wedding present can you buy with R5?'

I spent a very depressing afternoon with the books. The crippled teaboy and the insolent driver had been invited, and not me. Didn't she know who I was? That even Heidi came to me when the Greenbergs needed priming for a promotion she wanted to try?

But I never let on I was miffed. I still joined them on the break, pretending nothing was wrong. Most days, though, I got indigestion from the freshness in that room. Heidi would pour Hala's tea, and they'd talk about the play at the Nico Malan and act like they'd all played marbles together as children. Like you could sit with a kaffir and not notice he's stuffing chips into a loaf of bread and dunking it in his tea. But the Germans, we all know, have a thing for dark meat, and there were plenty stories of Heidi's skirts up with coloured men.

A week before the wedding, an announcement over the speakers summoned everyone to the main floor and, with the R300 collected, Heidi presented Hala with a dinner service from everyone at the factory. There were biscuits and speeches, and I stood there grinning, amazed at the lavishness of the gift. My wedding present 30 years ago – of course, there'd only been ten of us then – had been a satin nightie in tissue wrap, and here a girl who hadn't been at Rolaine's long enough to get used to the soft toilet paper was the recipient of a magnificent gift. Why? Probably a white designer with ten months' service would've gotten a lace tablecloth.

'Hala, can you come with me a minute, please?' Mr Saul asked the designer when everything was over and workers had returned to their posts.

I had to pick up the orders from Miss Rathbone in the front, and followed at a reasonable distance, watching Hala enter the corner office with Mr Saul.

Miss Rathbone hadn't attended the presentation and was on the telephone speaking to a buyer. I pointed to the folder on the desk. She could've handed it to me, but made me wait until she'd finished a speech about the popularity of ostrich feather trim.

Looking around at the samples hanging against the wall, I heard a commotion next door. Then the door flew open, and out came Hala, with Mr Saul nipping at her heels.

'Miss Baker, I didn't mean — '

He didn't know we were there, and charged by Rathbone's booth. At the front desk he caught up with her and grabbed her arm. Then a curious thing happened. As I say time and time again, but no one listens to me any more – give them too much, and this is what you can expect. Hala stopped, grabbed the sugar bowl from the secretary's tea tray, and flung its grainy contents into the guts of the IBM typewriter on the desk. She ran past the receptionist, out the door, and was gone. The audacity!

When all the talk had died down and a new designer was fending off advances, I was going through my accounts payable folder one afternoon when I found, stuck between two overdue accounts, a gold-edged invitation neatly addressed to Mrs B.

For the smell
of the sea

The first time I met Ezz she was lying in five inches of water in an old porcelain tub. 'Go in,' Hans, her 60-year-old artist-lover, said. 'Everyone else is in there.'

I followed Riaana into a narrow, white-tiled bathroom with this ponytailed man sitting on the toilet drinking beer, a very dark girl with long black hair and a short leather skirt on the edge of the bath smoking a joint, and this long-limbed Amazon with an ugly stomach scar distorted under the water lying back with a glass in her hand, her partial denture in a cloud of Steradent next to a tray holding pills, hair straightener, ointments, a douche bag and a biscuit tin brimming with lipsticks, shadows and blush.

'Shit, it stinks in here,' Riaana said.

'You are in a toilet, love,' Ezz smiled. 'So you have the nerve to visit after not pitching up for Hans's show at the gallery? And who's this?'

'My cousin, Sabah, on holiday from Canada. Sabah, this is Ezz, her cousin Myrna, and Myrna's boyfriend, Jeff.'

There was no place to sit so I leaned against the wooden door, careful not to skewer my neck on the nail, my eyes flitting briefly to the bubbles fizzing up between Ezz's legs, the smell punctuating the already rotten air.

'I love your hair,' she turned to me. 'Is it real?'

'Yes,' I laughed, surprised.

'Ezz hates her kaffir hair,' Jeff said. 'She can't accept her Bushman beginnings.'

'Oh, shut up, you. And look who's talking. The boy who broke off his engagement because Mommy said the girl's too dark, the children might come out black.'

I liked Ezz immediately, and tried to figure out the German artist who didn't mind this flagrancy. Ezz was young, a decade younger than me, with lively eyes, full lips, a solid body with mango breasts. It wasn't hard to figure the attraction.

The door pushed against my back.

'Maurice is on the phone.'

'Did you meet fishpaste Arthur yet?'

'You know I hate that name, Ezz.'

Arthur was tall, lantern-jawed, with pencilled eyes, an effeminate lilt in his voice.

'Maybe you'll stop blowing those old queens behind the Luxurama then. Look at that bruise in your neck.'

'You're a bitch, Ezz.'

'Oh, stop moaning like a baby. Tell Maurice I'll call him back. And wash your hands before you make the tea.'

Arthur reversed out the door.

Ezz got up and Myrna handed her a towel. She let out a tiny, smelly fart.

'Oh, stop it.'

'You know I can't help it.'

'Stop blaming it on the op.'

Jeff got up, and wrinkled his nose. 'Shit, what did you eat? Apricots?'

'I'm giving a dinner party next Saturday,' she turned to me. 'You must come.' And with that she went out into the dining room, where Hans was putting finishing touches to a painting, and led him into the bedroom, leaving us standing there to entertain ourselves.

On the way home Riaana filled me in. Ezz was a fitness instructor at a gym, and had met Hans at a jazz session when she was sixteen, ten years ago, dropping out of school and moving right into his flat. People popped in at all hours at her house, and it wasn't at all unusual on a weekend for someone to knock on Ezz's door at 4 a.m. – usually Jeff and his friends, Rollie and Ivor – too drunk to drive home from a party, and needing a place to crash. Sometimes five people were heaped up in the same room with Ezz and Hans. Nothing going on, of course. For all Ezz's big mouth and exhibitionism she was quite a prude. Her thing was having other people smell her farts. Once she'd had a whole bunch of friends watching television with her on her bed, then got up and locked the door so they couldn't escape.

Myrna and Jeff was another story, Riaana said. Supposedly they were just friends but Myrna, who was a publisher of an underground magazine, had a crush on Jeff. The problem was that Jeff had been on the lookout for the right-complexioned girl to please his mother, and wanted only sex. One poker night at Ezz's house, after too much brandy, he lost the game and did the wild thing with Myrna from one end of the living-room floor to the other, in front of everyone. In the morning Myrna was gone and Jeff was passed out with his false teeth out of his mouth.

I'd forgotten what Cape Town dinners were like, and turned up on the appointed night in Sussex Street, with my cousin, in a T-shirt and jeans. Ezz wore something that could only be likened to a black Spandex stocking showing every dimpled curve and leaving nothing to the imagination. Myrna was in a silver-studded top and pants. With her decked out and grand, and jazz on the stereo, if it hadn't been for Hans in his sandals and shorts, I would've felt like Aspoestertjie before the ball.

'So what do you think of all this new stuff going on, and the blacks coming into power?' Rollie Thomas asked. Rollie had come with Jeff, and had just brought them up to date on the elections scheduled for the following year.

'The sanctions worked,' I said.

'Have you been down to Sea Point yet? Or Camps Bay? You can't even get a spot to put up your umbrella or stretch your feet without getting sand kicked in your face.'

'I haven't been to the beach, but I've seen District Six. It's flattened like a pancake. At least they left the churches and mosques.'

'It's a ghost of a place,' Ezz agreed. 'Empty and desolate, with the wind blowing through everything. And all those people pushed for nothing into council homes on the Cape Flats. The whites are scared to move in. They know what it meant to us.'

Hans nodded. 'They say when the southeaster blows and you stand in Caledon Street, you can hear the ghommaliedjies and the cries of the people who used to live there.'

'When they demolished it, they killed the spirit of the people,' Riaana said. 'They took away the heart of the coloureds and the Cape Malays.'

'I don't like those words. "Coloureds" and "Cape Malays". That's their words for us.'

'I'm using it for practicality,' Riaana said. 'How would you classify your status?'

'Why do I have to have a status?'

Riaana didn't have an answer, and Jeff spoke. 'Well, at least you can call yourself a Canadian. I wouldn't tell anyone over there where I was from.'

'Actually, I feel very strongly about being South African.'

'Really?' Myrna said. 'So you didn't shed that along with everything else?'

I didn't quite know what she was trying to say. I was about to respond when Ezz spoke.

'Canada's played a big part in helping South Africa. Without the sanctions, it might not have happened. So we're grateful to the Canadians. Not like those kaks across the border from them who make noises to show their support but keep their hands on their balls. If this was Israel, you would've seen this place shaken up long ago.'

'Is it difficult to get into a squatter camp?' I asked.

'It's quite dangerous,' Myrna said. 'Why?'

'I was thinking of taking a look.'

'Taking a look? It's not an amusement park.'

'Don't be so hostile, Myrna,' Jeff said. 'She's just asking.'

'I saw a documentary on television the other day. Seven-year-olds giving their feelings and views. I couldn't believe what I heard.'

'You never knew?'

'I couldn't believe a seven-year-old talking about the darkness of South Africa. Only seven years old.'

There was an uncomfortable silence.

'You've been away a long time,' Hans said.

'And you know what they say about us, the ones in the middle – do you think we could've helped? I mean, we did get it better than them.'

'God, I hate this.' Myrna plunked down her glass. 'Suddenly everyone has a conscience. Next thing you'll tell us you're coming back to help.'

'I *am* coming back.'

'There. What did I say?'

'Not everyone left of their own accord,' Riaana offered.

'What do you mean?' Ezz asked.

'I don't think Sabah wants to discuss it. And she's always talked of coming back.'

'Why?'

'It's home.'

'It's dysfunctional.'

'Aren't we all a little fucked up, then?'

'Speak for yourself,' Myrna said.

'Hey, hey,' Ezz cut in. 'This is getting out of hand. Sabah's my guest here.'

'It's all right. I'd feel the same about any born-again, returning expat. But, show me a South African who hasn't suffered some kind of identity crisis, and I'll show you someone who's bought the plan.'

'Maybe. But you didn't take advantage of your white skin? Tell me the oppression you felt.'

'You know what I think?' Hans asked Ezz.

'What do you think?'

'I think this is turning into one of our *beat the visiting expat into a corner for running away* confrontations. Remember what happened to Chris two months ago? We should stop now. Sabah didn't come here to be interrogated.'

'It's all right,' I said. 'But do you know what I'm tired of, Myrna?'

'What?'

'I'm tired of this singsong over who's more oppressed. Black people aren't the only ones. We've had it better than them, yes, but we've suffered also. We can't dwell on and on. At least, if you're black, you know you're black. You're not tempted to get into the white section of the train because you'll get a seat, and you won't leave out your race on a job application because you're qualified and want the job. Who do I send the bill to for the last 40 years? De Klerk? Damn fucking skippy, I'm coming back.'

'Arthur, dessert!' Ezz shouted, although Arthur was right next to her.

'Shit, Ezz, you don't have to scream in my ear.'

'Give Sabah a cigarette.'

'I quit.'

'A rye and Coke.'

'I don't drink.'

'Well, something, then,' Ezz said. 'And you,' she said, turning to Myrna, 'you should listen to people before you open your fat mouth.'

'Excuse me? Your foot's still in yours from poking your nose into Gerald's business last week.'

'Your poes, man.'

'Did you see my poes?'

'Yes. You should start wearing underwear.'

'This is how the majority of people feel, though, Sabah,' Hans said. 'Returning South Africans are opportunists. Coming back to ride the wave. To live amongst the elite with their dollars and pounds, lording it over the rest.'

'Not everyone, Hans. Some of us never left. There's prejudice all over, even in Canada. Only here, they call it apartheid and everyone acts like we invented segregation.'

'In Canada, a citizen can vote irrespective of his colour,' Myrna said.

'Who's arguing? I'm saying, move on. If Mandela can forgive, why can't we give up sucking on it like an old tit? Now if you tell me I don't have a say because I left, well … that's not an argument – it's emotional.'

'Isn't this whole argument emotional?'

'Oh, for Christ's sake. Would you stop it already?' Ezz knocked her elbow into Myrna. 'Why do you want to come back, Sabah?'

'For the smell of the sea.'

'That's it?'

'I left my soul at the foot of Table Mountain. I want it back.'

For a few moments no one said anything. Then Ezz spoke again. 'I understand how you feel. We take this place for granted. Look how many times we said we'd leave – oh fuck, you're crying.'

'See what you did, Myrna?' Jeff accused. 'Jy hou ook nie op nie. Jy bly met die Canadians. Sabah, do you want to go outside?'

'I'm fine.'

'I'm sorry,' Ezz said. 'We shouldn't have attacked you like this.'

'You didn't attack me. This is what I know. What I miss. Why I want to come back.'

'And you will come back, and we'll have more nights like this. Arthur, did you make the tea?'

'Jy order net,' Arthur mumbled, going back out with the tray.

Myrna went to the sideboard for a pack of cards. 'Poker, anyone?'

'Strip?' Rollie asked.

'We can play strip, but we'll stop at the shirt,' Ezz said. 'None of that nonsense of the last time.'

Hans lit a joint, Myrna put out the peanuts and chips. I had a chance to think. Back in Canada a few weeks later, I revisited the conversation in that room many times when I saw my country's unrest unfold on the television screen. Sometimes I hear Ezz's laughter and see Hans's hand steal up her thigh, and feel the fires of Africa warm my bones. I stayed, that night, drugged with life, until my clothes reeked of smoke and Myrna was down to her serviette underwear.

Don't mention it

My grandmother was coming, and for weeks I listened to the excitement in my mother's voice whenever she spoke to Marcy on the telephone. Out went my panties with the holes and my brother's heelless socks, kitchen cupboards were cleaned out and wiped, cans and jars neatly stacked with labels all facing the front. I only knew my father's mother, who took us to the Sheraton to hunt for Easter eggs and bought us ribbed sweaters at Christmastime, and dreaded meeting this other grandmother who was coming all the way from the jungle to see what her Canadian grandchildren were about.

I'd heard stories about upbringing in South Africa. 'My mother would put chillies in my mouth if I said "damn"' or 'I'd get the hard end of the feather duster on my knuckles if I took what wasn't mine.' I knew my brother, whose mouth constantly runneth over, wouldn't have much of a chance, and I was counting on him to take most of the heat. But I was curious, anxious for clues about my own Mom, who I had long ago decided defied regular description. My brother and I were the only children in Richmond Hill who had a mom with a haircut like that rifleman with his boot on an elephant's head advertising cigarettes in *TV Guide*, who never stood up for *O Canada*, popping peanuts into her mouth while eyes

burned holes into the back of our heads. I was really curious to see
what kind of mother she had.

Finally the afternoon arrived, and my brother and I stood in our
pressed clothes at the airport waiting for my grandmother to come
through the electronic door, my mother leaning against a pillar
reading one of her short-story books. At my friend Louise's house
there were fashion magazines in the toilet; in ours, Nadine
Gordimer and Alice Munro; and on Mom's bed, where Dad used to
sleep, a stack of *Quarry* and *Grain*.

I knew the minute I saw this big woman in a cream, tailored suit
with this black velvet turban sitting a little crooked on her head, a
bright orange patch of hair sticking out the left side, that this was
my famous Gran. You didn't have to be an expert or anything to
know just from that patch that no one in their right mind would
pick a colour like that. Right there a piece of the puzzle fitted.

I was quiet that first day, chomping on a stick of dried meat
called biltong, listening to my mother shamelessly ransacking my
grandmother's brain for news of cousins and uncles and old friends,
watching the poor woman fight to stay awake – she'd waited four-
teen hours on a plastic chair for a connecting flight in Rome. Finally
my mother showed her to the extra bed she'd put in my room
upstairs. I hadn't looked forward to sharing, but was fascinated by
this big woman on the edge of the bed folding everything in a neat
pile on the chair, her suitcase open at her feet like at an Indian
bazaar displaying chocolates and dried fruit and slippers, and
guavas from the tree in her yard stuck between rolled clothing. I
was strangely comforted by the pleasantness of her eau-de-cologne.

'My girl, can you take my nightie out? It should be right on top.
Under those Cadburys, I think.'

'Yes, Gran.' I fairly hopped out of bed. 'This one?' I held the
pink brushed nylon one up.

'That's it. Thank you.'

'You're welcome.'

'You're welcome?'

'It means, like, well, when someone says "thank you," you say "you're welcome."'

'Oh, sort of like "don't mention it"?'

'Don't mention it?'

'Yes, don't mention it, it's a pleasure. You can also just say "pleasure." Someone says "thank you," and you say "pleasure."'

'I like "don't mention it" better because sometimes, Gran, don't you think, it's not always a pleasure?'

She laughed.

'You're right. I think that's why we say "don't mention it" most of the time. It's not always a pleasure. Smart Canadian tutus I have, I see.'

'Thank you, Gran.'

'You're welcome.'

We both got a kick out of that, and I got into bed, Gran pulling the covers up to my chin, kissing me on the head. I had already decided that since Juaa was Mom's pet – she denied this strenuously, saying he was just her first child – I would do everything to get myself in good with Gran. I knew, of course, like I always knew when people met my brother for the first time, that my grandmother too would be helpless under his spell. And she was, although she was a lot smarter than Mom at keeping it in the corner of her heart. But I had other strengths and, given time, knew I could prove myself. If there was one thing I knew like I knew I hated Gideon Cohn in my class, it was that my brother wouldn't be able to hold himself in for a whole two months.

When two weeks had passed, and I had warmed to the smells of puddings and fudge, because Gran had a thing about being idle and was always fussing in the kitchen whipping up treats, or in the living room with her feather duster – she'd brought one in her suitcase – I came to the conclusion that grandmothers were more fun than moms. Of course, she wasn't anything as glamorous as my other grandmother – Mom browned that orange hair fast and virtually wrenched away the eyebrow pencil, giving her eye-shadow instead – but then my Toronto grandmother didn't know baking powder from flour and bought cheesecake from a German baker, taking it out of the box before visitors arrived. That's not to say, though, that Gran's eyes and ears weren't in the best working order and that she didn't spot our little mistakes. Juaa got a hard taste when he came home with his bat one day after supper had been on the table an hour and was asked if he thought he was at a hotel. For a minute I thought he was going to roll those big eyes and turn on that smile that all those ten-year-olds liked, but he must've pitched some bad balls with his friends because he mumbled something unintelligible and went to the bathroom to wash his hands.

'Gran's talking to you,' my mother said, under pressure to exert some control.

'Whoa! I'd better listen, then.'

Mom threatened him with no supper, something she'd never done before, and my grandmother rolled those heavy legs of hers out of her seat, disappointment thick in her voice. 'I never thought I'd have a rude grandchild.'

That was all it took. My brother has this terrible problem. He can't function if he thinks you don't love him, even though he doesn't shut his mouth when he should, and the next morning, when Gran woke up, there it was on her folded slacks, a box of Smarties and a note. That the box was half-empty didn't matter; Gran was knocked over by the thought. When he returned from

school she'd made a trifle and he invited three of his friends to
come and meet his South African gran. From that day on it didn't
matter what he did – except backchatting Mom, of course – Gran
would just nod her head, and say, 'Ag.'

Around this time I noticed Mom, who had a rule about wanting everything in its place, getting edgy with Gran. Gran came
from a country, she said, where people knocked on your door for
a slice of bread, and one couldn't throw anything out. Leftovers
appeared everywhere. In one of Mom's china cups in the cupboard
was a handful of tangerine pips, turning the bottom of the cup
brown, that Gran was drying out to take home and plant because
'Florida naartjies were sweet'. In the fridge was an uncovered
saucer with half a boiled egg smelling up the cheese, a slice of
tomato, a half-eaten muffin, and farther back, behind the diet mar-
garine, a chicken wing in wax paper not properly sealed, and
crumbly sponge cake from the week before. Gran would begin an
O'Henry chocolate, lose interest, and save it for later on. The fruit
bowl in the kitchen had candy wrappers stuck between the
oranges and bananas. Gran never finishing anything.

'Mom, what're you saving these bits and pieces for?' My
mother would try to keep the sting out of her voice. 'Throw it out
if you can't finish it, please. I'm not short on tomatoes and eggs,
and chocolates you can do without.'

Personally, I didn't know what all the fuss was about. Gran was
a pack rat and loved to hoard, and had probably been a caterpillar
collector like me. And there was no mystery anymore about where
I got the habit of saving my meat for last on my plate till my potatoes and peas were gone. In any event, Gran would look at Mom
with doleful eyes, nod, then find a different hiding place. Mom, of
course, knew nothing about the stash of teabags growing mould in
a bowl under the bed. Gran was saving them to mix with her

henna paste, for she had every intention of going back to being a carrothead.

One afternoon, watching her iron sheets and underwear, I told her Mom just folded the sheets and smoothed out the panties with her hand.

'Your Mom never wore creased panties or petticoats, but I guess she's too busy now. But you put this on after your bath tonight, and tell me if it doesn't feel good against your skin. Women put on a little perfume sometimes to cheer themselves up, you know. A nicely pressed blouse or slip can do the same thing.'

'Really, Gran?'

'Really. But I notice people here don't care very much how they look. Not too many creases in pants or pleated skirts. Maybe that's why they're so out of sorts. Even your mother doesn't iron her jeans.'

'You only notice Mom's clothes now, Gran? She gets into trouble all the time at work because she hates wearing a dress.'

'But I see her wearing dresses and skirts.'

'Not Fridays, Gran. Fridays she wears jeans.'

'Jeans in an office?'

'She says she doesn't have to go in every day, and if they want her to bring in the business she's written Thursday night, it's jeans or they can wait till Monday. Of course, the manager wants the numbers on the board, so he has no choice, because Mom writes the most business, and if you say anything to Mom, you know how she is, she just won't write anything at all, even though it means we'll all be starving to death.'

'Starving to death? I don't think she'll do that,' Gran smiled. 'But your mother's always been a mischief-maker.'

'Tell me, Gran, did they really move her from Sub A to Sub B when she started school?'

'Yes. And when she was ten, she was Spring Queen. Make your Gran a nice cup of tea and I'll tell you about the time someone pulled her plait and she broke the girl's arm.'

'Gran, you're telling lies!'

'She didn't mean to, of course, but there it was, the girl called her whitey and pulled her hair, they rolled to the floor, and when they were separated by the teacher who'd come back into the class, your mother's mouth was bleeding and the girl's arm was broken.'

'Were they expelled?'

'No. But I got a call from the principal.'

'Did Mom tell you what happened?'

'She never said a word, and made up some story about a missing tooth. The tea, my girl? Do you remember how?'

'I boil the water, and make sure it boils.'

'Then you take that small white teapot with the pink flowers and put some hot water in it to warm it up.'

'I know the rest, Gran. You want the thin cup with the gold rim: you don't drink tea out of mugs. And three teaspoons of loose tea in the pot.'

'You forgot something.'

'Boil the milk in the microwave.'

'Right.'

I made it, hot and strong the way she liked, and put the two china cups next to the dainty plate of marzipan cookies she'd set out. I prayed my brother wouldn't come crashing through the door, and Gran drop everything to make him something to eat: there were things I wanted to know. But I'd hardly reached for a marzipan when I heard the bicycles slam against the wall, the front door open, and three of them tumble into the house.

'Gran, you remember Gregory and Mike? My grandmother

makes the best grilled-cheese sandwiches, guys! Can you make us some, Gran?' And before she could answer, they charged up the stairs to his room, our little tea party at an end.

Gran was restless and we were always out. 'You're just a street Arab, Mom,' my mother would say when Gran got fidgety.

'Well, I didn't come here to sit on my bum. I want to see Canada. Take me somewhere in the car.' So if it wasn't a movie or a restaurant or a drive to Niagara Falls, it was scouring the stores in the mall. And a most painstaking thing it was, as Gran had to examine every label, every price, to compare with the clothes back home.

The first time we took her to Bulk Barn, it was like witnessing someone who'd never been to a zoo with more than five animals. Gran saw all the barrels and bins and said that they could never have such a place in South Africa, people would just dip their hands in and steal. She loved the idea of taking as little or as much as you wanted in a plastic bag, and not being stuck with a five-pound bag of flour when you only wanted to make a few scones. Admiring the faith the shop owners had in their customers, Gran stood a bit too long in one of the aisles. I went to investigate. I saw her take a plastic bag and dip her hand into a barrelful of those big imported dates, putting three in the bag. Then, when we were pushing the cart down the aisle and no one was around, she removed the dates from the bag and put them in her pocket, leaving the empty bag in the cart. I couldn't believe it.

In the car going home, she took them out of her pocket and gave one each to me and to Mom. My mother said she didn't remember paying for dates, and Gran said she'd taken them as samples to see if she wanted to buy some the next time.

My mother was alarmed. 'That's stealing, Mom. You taught us stealing was wrong.'

'G'wan, man.' Gran took a bite on her date. 'They won't miss two or three. Look how much you paid for those cashew nuts.'

I must say, I liked Gran's philosophy. Not long after that, I'm sorry to say, Mom tried the same stunt with the cashew nuts. The difference was, whereas Gran eventually bought a few pounds of the dates to take back to South Africa, Mom just put a handful of cashews into her pocket, not even bothering with the plastic bag.

As one week slipped into another, and I saw the suitcase slowly fill up, I dreaded the end of August. Sometimes, when I watched from the other end of the dining-room table where I sat with my books, I caught Gran staring out at the lake. She was missing home, anxious to return, and I loved her for not sharing this with Mom. Gran knew. My mother didn't want to be here, but she was here because we were here and we had to be here because we were Canadian, my father said, and no one could take us away.

'What you sitting looking so glum for, Mom?'

'I'm just thinking, Sabah, my girl. You live so far away.'

'Yes, Mom.' And I picked up that thing in her voice.

'Are you ever going to come home?'

'One day, Mom.' She put a plate of cookies on the table, going back into the kitchen for the tea tray and a new short-story book.

Gran understood. And there was nothing I could do. When Mom would be the child and Gran would be the mom they communicated in a language of silences alien to me.

The last week of her stay, Gran decided to make balloon curtains for the whole house and she and my mother went over to this material place and aggravated the lady there for almost the whole afternoon. I hid behind the crêpe de Chine as I listened to my grandmother work out the lengths and widths of lace and taffeta from a scrap of paper she rooted out of her bag, the poor Chinese lady struggling to keep up as they decided first on one then

another colour, before dragging her to the other side of the floor
for something else. My mother had never had a needle in her hand,
but because she had now laid out $300 for a sewing machine,
while Gran was ordering the lady about, she was paging through
pattern books, fired up with how much money she could save. I
think I saw the lady cringe when Mom looked at the name tag on
her dress, and said, 'Big San, you've been so helpful. If I have any
trouble, I'll come straight to you.' We left laden like camels with
materials and zippers and patterns to keep Mom through
Thanksgiving the next year.

The living room took on a new look. The oak table was cleared
of the elaborate flower arrangement and in its place came the Elna
and metres and metres of dark green taffeta Gran fed through the
machine. The dtzzz dtzzz dtzzz was very soothing as it mixed with the
sounds of CJRT, the sun spilling onto Mom on the carpet, where
she was bent over a pattern like a girl cutting pictures out of a
colouring book.

'Oprah's coming on, why don't we take a break?'

Gran had become fascinated with afternoon talk shows. I'd
already had to grapple with a new word when Gran had said 'kaffir',
and Mom almost washed out her mouth, when here was another.

One of the ladies on the panel said she'd never had an orgasm,
and Gran asked what an orgasm was.

'What do you mean, what's an orgasm, Mom?'

'Well, I mean – do I know about these things?'

'What do you mean you don't know? At 56 you don't know
what an orgasm is?'

I could see that ridge hardening between Gran's eyes and
wished someone would fill me in.

'Well, you don't have to excite your liver about it, and stop
mentioning my age.'

'But Mom, you were married, for heaven's sake!'

Gran put her foot down with a vengeance on the treadle and fed the material through the machine.

'Do we have all these people coming on television in South Africa, spilling their guts, educating us? I don't need a man in my bed, and I'm sorry I blinkingwill asked.'

I went into the kitchen, made a pot of tea and took the tray into the lion's den, where Oprah was still philosophising.

'You want sweetener or real sugar, Gran?'

'Real sugar, please,' she said, knowing that this would sour Mom, who'd tried to cut her size with grapefruit and oat bran and twenty-minute workouts, so much so that Gran, caught up in Mom's mania to be thin, stood every morning on the bathroom scale with gown and slippers, waiting to see the pounds drop off. Of course, it didn't make a dent in those rolling thighs, and when the needle seemed stuck at 170, she said the seven pounds lost had gone straight from her face, and then ate real breakfasts when Mom left for work.

'Strong and hot, just the way I like it,' she smiled. 'Thank you.'

'Pleasure, Gran.'

Mom shot me a look that was hard to gauge, but she was properly chastised. Gran could've stuck matchsticks into avocado pips on the kitchen sill, she wouldn't have said anything.

The day of departure, we drove like mourners to the airport. After the plane was swallowed up by the clouds, I had my first rub with loneliness, and a whole new fix on Mom. Mom wasn't such a strange bird. Not after you met Gran. Struggling to break free from the pattern that had strangled her mother's life, she wanted us independent, but not so that we thought we didn't need love, 'cause that was Mom's problem now. She didn't read novels, she said, because that manipulated her time. *I was manipulated by the law,*

I won't be by a man. Relationships were short stories, good reads, where characters were lost on the moors or faded into sunsets.

My beloved grandmother came again in 1989 with her feather duster and orange hair. By this time, of course, Louise had had an orgasm in Greg's car, and I knew all about how Gran had missed nothing at all.

Where did you live
in Cape Town?

The cold bit into her ears, numbing them. She stood for a few more minutes leaning against the door of the car, watching other cars parking, more people arriving to take part in this most momentous event in the history of her beloved country. She got back into the car.

'Don't cry, Sabah.'

She had a box of tissues on the seat next to her. It was 7.30 a.m. There was no sun, but she was wearing sunglasses. She sat until she had calmed down, then tried again. This time she made it all the way down to the entrance of the brown stone building, but had difficulty holding back her tears. She returned to the car. Through the windscreen she watched the line start to form outside the building. She saw several people she knew. Even in the line-up to democracy, the Joneses stood with their own kind.

Whenever you take a fish out of water, Sabah, it's wet.

Why, Granpa?

Because some things never change.

This was the building in Toronto most South Africans would come to, to vote. Most for the first time. If she sat in the car long enough, she would see many of her friends. And others also with whom she had some kind of connection. She saw the dentist who took care of her mouth, with his wife. They were new to the city,

not yet Canadian citizens. They were in conversation with the
Goldsteins. They all lived on Bayview Avenue. Why had they left
South Africa now to come and live in this country?

There's no Islam in Canada, Sabah. Why are you going there?

Did I choose to go?

Another couple joined the line, Indian, and stood behind the
Goldsteins. Then she saw Mietjie Bassier, and his wife, Didja, and their
three grown children arrive in their blue Volvo. Mietjie, she knew,
wanted to go back home, but Didja didn't want to. Didja had learned
to play golf. She made a helluva lot of money working as a nurse.

Where did you live in Cape Town?

Why don't you just ask what I am?

She waited for a few more people to arrive. She didn't want to
speak to anyone she knew. She blew her nose, checked her appearance in the rearview mirror, and got out. This time she managed to
get to the line, not looking left or right. At last she was inside the
building. It was her first time in a place of voting. She looked at the
set-up. Several booths where you could cast your vote in private.
But who would she vote for? She had agonised over it. 'You must
vote for the ANC,' her other South African friends had said. 'You
can't take a chance with those white motherfuckers.'

The room was hot, the posters reviving another time. Table
Mountain receding in the distance. Her mother's white frock. How
was she standing there 27 years later with snow in her boots and
a pen in her hand? Her eyes misted, and she hardened herself. She
stared at the drop that fell on the form. Her hand wouldn't move.
She couldn't place her tick in any of the boxes on the form.

She started to walk away – past the Samsodien family, past the
De Bruyns, past Moena Daniels and her vibrant nineteen-year-old
daughter, who had an Italian boyfriend. Only when she was in the
safety of her car did she take off her sunglasses and burst out.

The new South Africa

Lady, that's the rules

Sabah arrived at the bank her mother had recommended, and stood for a moment studying the instructions on the steel door. Banks had come a long way since the sixties, when she was last there. Not all banks, but this one, certainly. You couldn't enter just by walking in. You stepped into an inner cubicle where, boxed in by glass, you waited for the red light to change to green, then went through another door into the bank. A robber might have his chance with a teller, but would think twice about being trapped in a glass booth on the way out.

Inside the bank, the line-ups were long – a row of tellers behind bullet-proof glass on the left, consultants in cubicles on the right. Sabah joined the line for the consultants and presently a girl with a name tag saying 'Esmeralda' pinned to the lapel of her navy blue blazer motioned for her to take a seat.

'I'm a returning resident. I'd like to open an account and transfer my money from Canada,' Sabah said.

'How long have you been out of the country?' Esmeralda asked.

'For 27 years.'

'You need a letter from Home Affairs.'

'I have dual citizenship. Here's a letter saying so. And here are my South African and Canadian passports.'

Esmeralda picked up the letter. 'The letter's six months old,' she said, after a cursory glance.

Sabah looked at the consultant in earnest. Esmeralda was a plumpish woman in her forties who looked like she'd had too much porridge that morning and now regretted it under her tight skirt. 'It is dated six months ago, but it doesn't change who I am. I'm a South African as well as a Canadian citizen. My birth certificate is more than 40 years old. Does that mean the information is incorrect?'

'You need a new letter, Miss.'

'Listen, Esmeralda, forget the letter,' Sabah said, trying to keep calm. 'I shouldn't have mentioned the letter. Here's my South African passport. I want to open an account.'

Esmeralda picked up the passport and studied it. 'This is an old ID number. They changed them when they came out with the Book of Life. Do you know what's a Book of Life? It's an identity document with your picture, identity number, and driver's licence. If you buy a firearm, that would be registered in there, too. Everyone must have a Book of Life.'

'I understand, but I've just arrived. A Book of Life isn't first on my list. In the meantime, I want to open an account and transfer my money from Canada. Before the season changes, Esmeralda.' She smiled to show that she wasn't upset.

Esmeralda didn't share her humour. 'The best thing is to go to Home Affairs and first get your Book of Life, Miss. When you have it, we can open an account.'

'Home Affairs takes three months to process identity documents,' Sabah said patiently. 'Just forget I showed you this letter. Forget everything I've told you, Esmeralda. I'm South African. Here's the proof. That's all I need to open an account. I want to open an account and transfer my money. Not sleep with the manager.'

A bright spot appeared on Esmeralda's cheeks. 'You don't have to get huffy with me, Miss.'

Sabah wasn't smiling any more. 'Do you think you could go and ask whoever's in charge of returning residents whether a South African passport's good enough to open an account in this bank?'

Esmeralda kicked back her chair with a flourish and went off. Sabah leaned back and closed her eyes. How often did a returning resident step into the bank to open an account, she wondered. And how many of them would even have a dual citizenship letter for Esmeralda to be so familiar with it that she could say it was too old to be of use?

Esmeralda returned and placed the letter and passports in front of her.

'The manager says you need a fresh letter.'

'I don't believe it.'

'You'll also have to fill out a form for the Reserve Bank. The application's R250.'

'What?'

'You're bringing dollars into the country. The Reserve Bank keeps track of all monies coming in.'

'I bring money into the country and I pay for the privilege? I've never heard of anything so ridiculous!'

Esmeralda smiled. She was feeling a lot better. 'That's the rules. Also, if we have to fax your bank in Canada to transfer the funds, it's 13 rand and 68 cents. There's a cover page, and a page with the message. That would come to ...' she hastily jotted down figures on a scrap pad, '27 rand and 36 cents.'

Sabah wanted to smack the look off her face. 'Does your bank do anything for its customers, Esmeralda? Anything at all for free? Or are they all too complacent because they have no competition?'

Esmeralda gave her a smug look. 'I can give you the name of the manager if you want to complain.'

'Don't bother. I'll take my business elsewhere.'

The morning with Esmeralda had depressed her and she left there for her brother's office. Fa'iq said they should try his bank, and the next day he went with her to the main branch at Wynberg, where she explained her position to a young woman in Foreign Exchange.

'I should tell you, Karen,' Sabah started, identifying the girl by the name tag on her green-flowered dress, 'that I've been to one of your competitors and was given a long story about the Reserve Bank and a letter from Home Affairs. I don't know what the big deal is about opening an account if a person has a South African passport.'

Karen was a fresh-faced blonde. She'd been with the bank ten years. 'When you left the country 27 years ago,' she asked, 'did you fill out a form at the bank and tell them you were emigrating?'

'No.'

'Then you don't need a letter from Home Affairs. We can open an account right away.'

Sabah slumped forward in relief. 'Thank God.'

'If you didn't sign any forms when you left, you didn't officially leave.'

'Why didn't the other girl ask me that question?'

Karen smiled. 'Maybe she didn't know. We listen to our customers.'

'Fa'iq, did you hear that? They listen to their customers.'

'However, there's no getting around the R250 for the Reserve Bank,' Karen continued.

'That's a lot of money for information I'm happy to supply for free.'

'How much money are you bringing into the country?'

Sabah scribbled a dollar amount on a scrap of paper and showed it to her.

Karen gave an even bigger smile. 'For that amount, I'm sure we can work out something.'

'What do you mean?'

'When it arrives, perhaps we can do something with the rate.'

'You can do that?'

'We can keep it in abeyance for a day or so – especially if it arrives on a Friday – keep it until the Monday and check the rate on that day. If it's in your favour, we'll give it to you. Of course, you won't get the two days' interest, but even a slight change in the rate can result in a few thousand rands' difference. It'll make up for the R250 charge.'

Sabah looked at her. 'I like you, Karen. And the fax to have the money transferred?'

'It's R9 a page. We won't charge you.'

Sabah smiled. 'Karen, I'm very impressed with this bank.'

Karen started to explain the various accounts. Half an hour later travellers cheques had changed hands, and an account for the incoming funds had been opened.

'Well, that's that,' Sabah said to Fa'iq when they were out in the car. 'What's next?'

'We should go to Home Affairs and apply for your Book of Life, and get it over with. But let's first go and have some hot chips. I know this place not far from here. They make the best.'

'One packet, we'll share.'

'One packet's too little. I'm hungry,' Fa'iq said.

'A packet and a half, then. I don't want all that grease in my arteries.'

'You and your arteries. Remember those fresh cream doughnuts we used to scoff two at a time?'

Sabah laughed. 'And I could eat a chicken sandwich right after that, and still weigh in at 110. Now, one piece of chocolate goes straight to my hips.'

They arrived at the take-out restaurant. Fa'iq asked for a packet and a half of peri-peri chips.

The girl, with a doek on her head and four missing front teeth, looked at him as if he had asked for the keys to the *Challenger*. 'A packet anna half? I dunno how many chips to give for a halfa packet.'

'Half of one packet,' Fa'iq said.

The girl shook her head. 'I have to ask Mr Singh.'

'You have to ask if you can sell us one and a half packets of chips? The chips is R4. You give us one packet, and a half of one packet, and you charge us R6.'

'I have to ask.'

'Forget it,' Fa'iq said, turning to go.

'No, don't forget it,' Sabah cut in, nodding to the people waiting patiently behind them. 'Let her get Mr Singh.'

Mr Singh was short and squat, with six strands of hair combed from one ear all the way over his speckled dome to the other. 'What's the problem?' he asked.

'We'd like some hot chips, please,' Sabah said. 'We want more than a packet, but less than two. We're not hungry enough for two packets. We'll pay for the extra chips.'

'I can sell you a parcel.'

'What's a parcel?'

'Viennas and chips.'

'We don't want Viennas, just chips,' Sabah said. 'We want one and a half packets. We'll pay the extra.'

The store owner moved aside and pointed to the chips bubbling in the fryer.

'Lady, you know how much it costs to heat this fryer? You want to see my 'lectricity bill? If I do it for you, I have to do it for everyone.'

'What're you doing? You sell chips. You make the rules. All we want is a packet and a half of your chips.'

A man stepped up from the line that had formed behind them. 'Lady, buy two packets, I'll take what you don't want.' He had a nervous tic and the corner of his mouth twitched as he spoke.

'I appreciate that, but there's a principle involved here.' Sabah turned back to the owner. 'Are you giving us the chips?'

Mr Singh wiped the sweat off his forehead with the back of his hand. 'I can't do it. It's one packet, or two.'

'I don't believe it,' Sabah said.

The man behind them lost control. 'Give de woman de focking chips!'

Mr Singh looked at the man with the tic glaring at him and gathered himself upright in an effort to make himself taller. 'Look here,' he sputtered.

'No, you look. We stan'ing here focking ten minutes. Give de woman de chips!'

'No. He can keep his chips,' Sabah said. 'He can fry that attitude and sell it.'

Fa'iq pulled her out of the store. 'What's the matter with you?'

'I've had it with this third-world turtle mentality. First the woman in the bank, now this idiot.'

'You're in Cape Town, get a grip. With Esmeralda, you ran into affirmative action. This guy's just a *poes*. Let's go and eat something before we hit Home Affairs. And let's go somewhere where we can sit down.'

'I can't take the government this afternoon.'

'Just get it over with. You'll feel better after you've eaten. I promise you. Otherwise you have to come back another day and start all over again.'

After a tuna salad sandwich at Cavendish Square, they headed for the Home Affairs office in Wynberg. Feeling somewhat restored, Sabah explained to a young woman with a mane of sun-bleached surfer's hair that she had lived in Canada for 27 years and wanted to apply for a Book of Life.

'No problem,' the girl smiled pleasantly. 'Fill out this yellow form here and have two photographs taken – do you have a driver's licence?'

'A Canadian one.'

'Oh. We can't put that into your Book of Life. You have to go to the Traffic Department, and have your licence converted, then return to Home Affairs and we'll incorporate it into your Book of Life. You can have your pictures taken at the side of the building. There's a photographer in a caravan parked in the driveway.'

Sabah had her picture taken and was at the Traffic Department within the hour. There, she went straight to a woman with a stiff bouffant and pointed spectacles, called Mrs Marais, smoking a cigarette behind a thick glass barrier. Mrs Marais listened to her relate what the woman at Home Affairs had said, then let out a slow, poisonous stream of smoke and sighed heavily.

'They don't know what they're talking about at Home Affairs. You first apply for your Book of Life. When you have it, you bring it here with your Canadian licence, pay R40, we convert it, then you take it back to Home Affairs and apply for a new Book of Life.'

Sabah frowned. 'I don't get it. You mean I apply for the same document twice?'

'That's right.'

'It doesn't make sense. Why don't I have my licence converted first, as the girl said, then take it to Home Affairs to have it incorporated into my Book of Life? That way I only apply for the Book of Life once. You surely don't mean it. There must be a mistake.'

'I've worked here 24 years,' Mrs Marais smiled tiredly. 'Believe me.'

'Who pays for my petrol to drive up and down? My time? The R40?'

'Lady, that's the rules.'

'The rules? I'm tired of the rules. People keep telling me about the rules. Who makes these rules?'

'You can write a letter to the ANC. It's a free country now, anyone can say anything. Maybe they'll change it.'

'The ANC made this rule?'

'Listen, let me call Home Affairs in Cape Town. I know someone in the office there. I'll hear what he says.'

Sabah and Fa'iq waited at the counter and watched Mrs Marais blow smoke circles as she nodded and sighed into the mouthpiece. 'He wants to talk to you,' Mrs Marais said after a while, handing the receiver to Sabah.

'Lady,' a guttural Afrikaner voice boomed in her ear, 'this is Mr van der Westhuizen. Home Affairs in Wynberg's got their wires crossed. Mrs Marais is right. You first get your Book of Life, then get your licence converted, then go back to Home Affairs with both documents and apply for a new Book of Life.'

'Mr van der Westhuizen, surely, this is a ridiculous rule. Isn't that rather like feeding the chicken before slitting its throat?'

The official laughed awkwardly. 'Someone made that rule, Miss. There's a reason for it.'

'That's what scares me. Someone actually sat down and made such a rule.' She handed the phone back to Mrs Marais.

Mrs Marais nodded sympathetically. 'Why did you come back to this country?' she asked.

'I like to be punished,' Sabah said.

Mrs Marais returned her documents. 'It's not so bad here, you'll see. Give it a chance. In no time you'll get used to it.'

Out in the car, Sabah leaned her head into her hands. 'I'm not going to Home Affairs.'

'You are,' Fa'iq said. 'We don't want to come here again tomorrow.'

At Home Affairs, Fa'iq filled in the forms and they joined the throng of people waiting in line. Three of ten clerks were at their stations to attend to 40 or more people, the wait so long that mothers sat on the floor breastfeeding their babies, while children ran up and down making a noise.

Finally, at 3:30, it was her turn to step up to the counter and spread out her forms. The clerk was a young, no-nonsense woman with the stub of a cigarette burning between yellowed fingers. She drew the last, precious poisons into her lungs, examined the documents, made several ticks, then looked up.

'It says here "divorced."' She pointed to the box where Sabah had made a tick. 'Do you have your divorce order with you?'

Sabah crunched her toes together in exasperation. She wanted to scream, but forced herself to remain calm.

'Miss, I've had a rough day. You won't believe how rough. A few days in the country and I'm inundated with rules. I don't carry my divorce papers around in my purse. Do you? Tick off "never married," I don't care. Please. If you don't do it, I'm not coming back.'

The clerk looked down at the form. A frown appeared in the freckled space between her eyes. To Sabah's utter disbelief, she scratched out 'divorced' and ticked off 'never married'. She never looked up. It never happened.

Sabah looked at her brother. A government employee with guts!

The woman stamped the documents and handed them back to her. 'That line over there,' she pointed. 'For your fingerprints.'

'My fingerprints? Why?'

'Everyone has to do it, Miss. It's the law.'

'My fingerprints is a personal thing. Why do they want it?'

The clerk pursed her thin lips. 'Because they do.'

'My fingerprints is like my period,' Sabah went on. 'It belongs to me. Not even the FBI has it. Why should I give it to Home Affairs?'

The clerk was already looking over her shoulder at the next applicant. The Home Affairs office was the war zone for liberalised expatriates who couldn't come to grips with the reality of being back. She was tired of their whining.

'If you don't have your fingerprints taken, you won't get your Book of Life.'

'But in Canada, we don't — '

'This isn't Canada. Now please, if you don't mind. This office is closing in twenty minutes. There's a long queue. Next!'

The person behind Sabah, a well-dressed woman with a tan, smiled understandingly. 'Don't take it so hard,' she said. 'I returned last year after fifteen years in Australia. This is my eighth trip to Home Affairs. They wrote to me to say I owed them 43 cents. It cost them 80 cents to mail the letter. Welcome back.'

The guilt

Lilian Thurgood was busy picking guavas at the side of the house when she heard the growling of the Alsatians on the stoep. Just a low growl telling her that someone had stopped at the gate. Perhaps it was the postman, she thought, dropping something into her box. She looked about for a moment. They were at the end of winter, the morning fresh with the footprints of rain. She marvelled at the brightly coloured tips of trees, the pots of purple and pink geraniums with cellophane drops glistening on the leaves, the cluster of basil and oregano sprouting near the lemon tree. She liked the mornings, when God's breath was hot on the earth and steam rose from it in easy surrender.

Then she heard the growling again. Low, more intense. Someone had stopped at the gate. She put down the basket with the guavas, and reached for her cane.

She reached the front of the house and saw Tembi and Tor like sentinels at the gate. Fierce and powerful dogs, they had been trained by her late husband, Jock, to follow specific commands. It was the man's calmness that held them back.

'Can I help you?' she asked.

'I am looking for work, Madam.'

'I don't have any work.'

He reached into a brown envelope and lifted out a plastic-wrapped sheet of paper. 'I am from the Transkei, Madam. I have here a letter.'

Lilian Thurgood looked at him. He was young, persistent, in dark pants and a jacket that had seen darning and letting out but was clean. She'd seen these letters before, but took it from him anyway. As she suspected, a letter on a homemade letterhead – the paper dirty, water-stained, dog-eared – saying William Sidlayi was collecting donations on behalf of some organisation. He was doubly prepared. If he couldn't find work, he would ask for a handout. The letter made it easier to beg.

She handed the letter back through the grille of the gate. The gate was locked, the wall round the property ten feet high.

'Wait here,' she said.

'Thank you, Madam.'

Lilian left him at the gate and started to walk to the house, listening for the renewed growls of the dogs.

In the house, she looked for change in her purse. She knew it was a mistake. She should've been hardened by now. Every day people knocked on her door for food, old clothes, money and work. Most days she didn't answer. They took merciless advantage, especially since the new government. There was a new boldness.

She remembered the African woman who'd knocked at her door one night at nine. She didn't want to go out. It was raining, and it was a long walk to the gate. But there was the woman, with a child on her back and one at her side. Did the madam have garbage bags? she called out. An unusual request, especially at that time of night. And Lilian couldn't see well in the dark. What if there was a second person waiting behind the wall with a knife or a gun? The papers were full of stories of people getting killed in their own gardens and houses, and she'd heard of husband-and-wife team crime waves.

She went to the gate. There was no one but the woman and her children, but it irked her that she should be afraid in her own home, that they thought it all right to knock on your door any time of the day or night. Was it racist if you were afraid and didn't want to open your door to strangers? But, of course, she knew what it was. It was making good on the guilt, the guilt they were accused of having. As benefactors of the old regime, whites were shot through with guilt. And where there was guilt there was opportunity.

Like the woman who saw her sit on the stoep the other day and begged her to buy four geranium plants for R2. Her garden was overcrowded with flowers, but the woman insisted. If the madam would buy eight plants for R4, she would even plant them. Lilian had felt sorry for the woman and opened the gate. The woman threw herself to the ground with her grocery bags in which she kept the plants individually wrapped in wet newspaper, and asked for water so she could wet the ground. Lilian went round the side of the house for the hose, and when she returned, there was the woman with 30 plants in the soil. How she'd managed to plant so many in a few minutes, Lilian didn't know. 'Please, Madam,' the woman begged, 'it's almost five o'clock. I can't go home with these last few plants. Madam won't regret it, Madam will see. I'll even give Madam a special price, R12.' Lilian gave the woman the R12.

Then there was the man who rang persistently at her gate, and when she came out, asked for money for the bus as he didn't know how he was going to get home. When Lilian told him she had no money, he asked for clothes, and when she said she had none, he asked for food. But not brown bread, he added. Could he please have a tin of fish?

Lilian's thoughts returned to the young man waiting at the gate, and she fished around in her purse for loose change. There was only a R5 coin and 23 cents. R5 was a lot of money for a pensioner to give away, but she couldn't give him 23 cents. What could a grown man do with 23 cents? She was suddenly angry. Angry that she should be standing there examining her conscience. That she should feel guilt for his circumstances, and shame for the forged letter in his hand, for having to beg, for raising these emotions in her. She was a pensioner. What money did she have? If her husband had been alive, he would've ordered the man off the grounds.

She went outside and found him still at the gate trying to be friendly to the dogs. She gave him the R5 coin. He took the money, then vigorously nodded his head.

'I can't take this R5.'

'What do you mean?' Lilian asked, not understanding him.

'I can't just take Madam's R5. Let me do some work for it. I see Madam has many leaves from the trees on the grass. I can clean it up for Madam. I want to work for it.'

'It's all right. Take it. It's a donation, isn't it?'

'Yes, Madam, but it's R5. I can clean Madam's garden.'

'It's quite all right. Please.'

'No, Madam, I insist. Look over there, look at all those leaves.'

Lilian looked at the carpet of leaves covering half of the garden. She didn't have the energy to argue. 'All right,' she said, knowing herself to be foolish to open the gate.

William stepped in, and the dogs moved forward, pink tongues idling in readiness. Lilian made a signal and they relaxed.

'Your name is William?' She remembered the name on the letter.

'Yes, Madam.'

'William, just those leaves over there.'

'Does madam think I'm a skelm? That I want money for nothing? Those leaves are not even R2.'

'Well, just do R5 worth, then. Really, you don't have to do anything. I gave you the money. Just those leaves over there. I've got to
go out in a few minutes.'

'Don't worry, Madam. I'll be finished now-now.'

Lilian remained at the gate and watched him remove his coat as
if he were going to tackle the whole garden. She knew he knew
that she wasn't going anywhere, that opening the gate was more a
show of trust than a display of fearlessness.

The rake was under the guava tree and she watched him fetch
it and sweep up the fruit, sorting the good ones from the pile. He
would take them, he said, if she had no use for them. She said it
was all right and watched him collect curled fig leaves and other
debris, and stuff them into the bin.

'That's enough, William. Thank you. I really appreciate it.'

'No, Madam.'

'Really, it's all right. You've done enough.'

The telephone rang and Lilian excused herself. The dogs followed her into the house. She wouldn't lock the door behind her,
she told herself. She trusted him. She would show him that she did.
She wouldn't make him feel like a criminal. Black people knew that
white people were afraid of them. She would show by her actions
that she wasn't one of them. But what if she was wrong? What if
he came in after her into the house? The old revolver was in a box
at the back of the wardrobe, but she wouldn't even know what to
do with it.

Lilian reached the phone, but the caller had hung up. She
became aware of her pulse. Racing. Frantic. She stood for a minute
to calm down. The dogs growled. She turned. William was at the
door.

'Madam?' he said nervously.

'Yes?'

'I've raked the leaves and cleaned up the guavas.'

'Thank you, William. I'll unlock the gate for you now.'

'I've worked one hour, Madam. That's R10.'

The effrontery shocked her, but lasted only seconds. Lilian did something with her hand, and the dogs rose. 'I'll ask my husband for the money,' she said.

'There's no husband, Madam,' he said in a calm voice. 'Madam lives alone. Why's Madam so afraid? I'm not a thief. Madam will give me the money?'

Lilian's purse was on the mantelpiece and she reached for it. In front of him she took out a R10 note. The tone of his voice had changed, and somewhere deep inside her, she felt a terrible chill. She was painfully aware that the only thing between her safety and his will was the dogs.

'I only have this R10 note. You can give me back the R5 I gave you.'

'Madam wants change? I thought the R5 was a donation. Madam owes me R10 for the work I did.'

Lilian looked at him. The smile on his face told her that he thought her a stupid old woman. That she had no choice. Still, she could not get herself to give him the money. 'Leave my house, please,' she said.

'The R10, Madam.'

'Now, or I'll call the police.'

He came forward.

'Sa!' Lilian commanded the dogs.

The bitches leapt – Tembi at William's wrist, Tor at his collar – and knocked him to the floor. William screamed at the top of his lungs as the dogs ripped at his clothes and nipped with their sharp teeth at his hands and arms.

Lilian looked at him squirming under the canines. The Alsatians had their snapping mouths dangerously close to his face, slopping saliva all over him. They would terrorise but not draw blood, not until the other command. Lilian had never had to try that out on them yet. She didn't know what the dogs might do if she gave the last signal.

'Please, Madam, please!' William shouted. 'I'll leave!'

Lilian left him struggling under the dogs and went to her bedroom. In the wardrobe, she found the little brown box behind Jock's army paraphernalia, and drew out the revolver wrapped in its piece of green felt. It was heavy, smooth, and she stroked it with her fingers, strangely calmed, aware of the screams in the front room. She couldn't remember whether Jock had said it was the revolver or a pistol that had a safety, and couldn't remember how to check if the chamber was loaded. There were no bullets in the box. Gripping her hand tightly about the weapon, she limped out. There was a tremendous surge of something pumping through her veins. She wasn't Lilian Thurgood. She was a woman possessed by only one thought: to live. In that moment she understood that it took very little to pull a trigger, and that the distance between sanity and insanity was no distance at all.

'The law says I can shoot if you trespass on my property.' She pointed the gun down at him.

William's eyes danced around in his head like cherries in a slot machine. His jacket was in shreds, the front of his shirt and face wet with snot and dog spit.

'Please, Madam! … don't shoot!'

She tightened her finger on the trigger.

'It would be good for some old woman who's afraid to sleep with her windows open, to read what I've done, William.'

'No, Madam!!'

Lilian Thurgood loomed over him, pointing the gun at his

head. For a frightening moment she felt trapped in a vacuum and couldn't move. The moment passed and she stared down at the gun trembling in her hand. She snapped a command. The dogs took their paws off his chest.

'Get up, and put the R5 I gave you on the table,' she said.

William struggled up onto his feet. He felt his jacket, but there was no pocket left.

'It's in your pants,' she said.

He slipped his hand into his trousers and took out a handful of silver.

'Just what is mine. Put it on the table.'

William did as he was told.

'Now walk backwards out the door so I don't have to shoot you in the back.'

With the dogs nipping at his knees, William reversed gingerly out the door, tiptoeing backwards down the stone path to the gate. Lilian had the gun pointed at him, her eyes never leaving his face.

'I'm going to report you to the police, William. I'm going to give them your description and tell them about the scar under your left ear, about the letter you walk around with, about your evil little scheme to get yourself on someone's premises. I'm going to report you not because I think they're going to catch you, but because I'm going to shoot you if you come here again.'

She unlocked the gate and watched him edge nervously out. William was wide-eyed, still expecting her to pull the trigger. Without a backward glance, he ran down to the main road, where he turned the corner and vanished from sight.

Lilian Thurgood stood very still. Her heart was racing, but the pain in her leg had disappeared. She looked about her. A woman pushing a pram with an infant in it passed her gate. 'Morning,' the woman said, smiling at her. Lilian couldn't speak. Her right hand shook and she put her left hand over it to still the trembling. She stood for a moment, then went inside. She didn't put away the gun, and didn't go to the medicine chest for her pills. She made a cup of tea and sat down at the kitchen table listening to the laughter and shouting of the children in the schoolyard across the road.

At three, Margaret and Ruth and Ethel May came over for the game of bridge they played on Wednesday afternoons. They commented on the high colour in her cheeks. Lilian said she'd been raking up the leaves. That night in bed, the gun in its new place under the pillow where Jock's head used to be, she cried softly into her hands.

Double storey

Nadia Williams sat in the waiting room of the gynaecologist's office, waiting patiently for her turn. How many fertility treatments she had had, how many failed attempts. She would miss her period, her breasts would become tender. She would even put on weight – only to have another false alarm. But this time she felt it was different. She hadn't had a period in two months, and had the strangest cravings for food, as well as an overwhelming nausea in the mornings. The lab had already taken her blood and urine. In minutes she would know from the doctor whether she was at last going to have a child.

The receptionist called her name and she went into Dr Julia Cohen's office. The doctor listened to her for a few minutes, then asked her to put on a gown in the adjoining room. She didn't have to examine her, she already knew the results of the tests. Nadia felt the cool hands on her abdomen, and tried to read from her expression if she could see anything there.

'You can get dressed,' she said, returning to her desk where she made notes in a file.

Nadia put on her top and came back into the office. The gynaecologist looked at her. 'I'm so sorry to tell you this, Nadia – you're not pregnant.'

The words had a numbing effect. Nadia sat down. She watched Dr Cohen's lips move, but heard nothing she said. She left the office, and started to walk. When she was almost in Wynberg she realised she was going the wrong way. She walked back towards Claremont. At her friend's coffee shop in the square, she broke down in the back room and told Soemaya what had happened. She and Soemaya had been friends since high school. Soemaya brought a pot of rooibos tea and honey and a buttered scone with thick cream. 'Talk to me,' she said.

Nadia stirred a teaspoon of honey into her tea. 'I don't know that I can continue with any more of these tests. It's two years now, and every time we have this hope when I miss a period, and every time it's nothing. This time I really thought I was pregnant.'

Soemaya reminded her of a mutual friend. 'Remember Galima? She also went through all of this. It took her ten years – treatment after treatment – and then they went on a holiday to Greece, and it happened.'

Nadia tried to smile. 'I'm 33. I don't have ten years. And we're not going to Greece. But if we know a trip will make it happen, we will go.'

'That's just it,' Soemaya said. 'You mustn't expect it, or go with that expectation. You put too much pressure on yourself.'

'It's hard not to think about it. Sedick says I mustn't worry so much about it, but I know he would like us to have a child. What man wants to be married and have no children? And he would make such a good father.'

Soemaya let her talk. Afterwards, she walked Nadia to a waiting taxi. 'I'll come and see you tomorrow,' she said, 'after I've closed the shop.'

That evening Nadia told her husband, Sedick. Sedick was a good husband. He loved his wife, and had told her many times that nothing would change between them if she couldn't have a baby. He held her while she cried.

When he came home from work the following evening, there was no supper. Nadia was lying on the couch staring at a television which wasn't switched on. Sedick opened a can of tuna, peeled an onion, and made sandwiches. He took the sandwiches and a pot of hot tea in to her on a tray. He sat on the side of the couch and they ate.

After a long silence, she spoke. 'I don't want to do these treatments any more.'

'I don't want you to either,' he said. 'We'll accept it. We have each other. That's enough for me.'

She turned to look at him. Her heart filled up with love. What a good husband he was. Caring, mindful of her feelings, always there for her. How could she let him down?

'I won't mind if you want to take a second wife,' she said.

Sedick put down his sandwich on the tray. 'Where does this come from?' he asked, putting his arms around her. 'I don't want a second wife.'

'I can't give you children, Sedick. I could never live with this guilt. It would be selfish of me to expect you to go through life without children. Every man wants to see what he can produce. You deserve to have children. Look how long we've tried.'

Sedick was quiet for a while. 'I love you. You're enough for me, Koeks. If we can't have children, it's God's will.'

'I know you say that, but will you still feel like that five years from now? In this case, and only in this case, I'm prepared to share.'

Sedick laughed suddenly. 'And just who did you have in mind for this?' he asked.

Nadia disentangled herself. 'Soemaya,' she said. 'She's never been married, she's attractive and smart, and we've been friends a long time. I could ask her. You like her, and she likes you. She's single, she understands these things. She might say yes.'

'You sound serious. You have to love someone to be able to do this.'

'You will,' she said, 'enough to. She's good looking, it won't be hard. But of course,' she added with a mischievous laugh, 'you will love me more.'

'Of course.'

'You can only have one koekie.'

He laughed.

For three weeks nothing more was mentioned. Nadia recovered a little from her setback, and slowly settled back into her routine. Sedick didn't want her to work. He earned enough money as an architect for her to stay home and do what she wanted, and she had a little sewing business in the staff quarters in the yard. She loved designing and bought imported fabrics, which lined one of the walls in big rolls. Two women sewed bridal gowns and made wedding accessories for her. The part she liked best was stitching on the beads. A wedding gown could have as many as two or three thousand tiny beads. She loved to sit in the wing chair in her lounge in the afternoon sun with a gown in her lap and a box of beads. She worked out her life dreams as she stitched.

After doing some particularly intricate beading on a cream satin outfit for a client, Nadia went to visit Soemaya at the coffee shop. It was after three in the afternoon, the lunchtime crowd had eased off. They sat under an umbrella in front of the shop drinking cappuccinos. Nadia spoke to her friend, fully expecting Soemaya to be shocked by her request.

'I have to think about it,' Soemaya said.

'You're not shocked that I've asked you such a thing?'

Soemaya's dimples deepened. Nadia noticed for the first time that her friend's hazel eyes looked almost green in the sun. 'No. I understand why you want to do it.'

'And you might be able to do such a thing?'

'I don't know. I'll make istigarah salaah. I'll ask Allah for guidance.'

Nadia left the coffee shop a little while later with mixed emotions. Her friend hadn't been as shocked as she had thought she would be, and hadn't found it at all strange that she had asked her to be part of a polygamous marriage. And she hadn't really thought about what might happen if her husband fell in love with Soemaya, and Soemaya with him. Soemaya would bear him children. She might lose Sedick. It was only after she had left the shop that she realised what she'd done. She said nothing to her husband of her visit to Soemaya. A few days later, over coffee at a mall in Tygerberg Valley, he brought up the subject himself.

'Did you ever speak to Soemaya?'

'About what?' she asked, knowing full well what he was referring to.

'You know – your notion about her becoming a second wife.'

She looked at him, feeling a little pang. 'I did.'

'What did she say?'

Nadia became aware of a new emotion within herself. Why was she upset when it had been her idea in the first place?

'She said she was going to make istigarah salah, to ask God for guidance.'

For two weeks Nadia made no contact with her friend. She was too afraid to call Soemaya for fear that the subject would come up. She

had made a terrible mistake, and the only way was to hope that it
would all somehow go away and be forgotten. But it wasn't to be.
She received a call from Soemaya one morning just as she was sitting down to have breakfast.

'I've made istigarah salaah,' Soemaya said. 'I've received guidance from Allah.'

'You have? Oh, you mean about *that*?'

'Yes. I've decided to do it. I'll marry Sedick.'

Nadia felt panic. She had proposed her friend as a second wife
for her husband at a time when she felt guilt and failure at her
inability to produce a child, but hadn't really meant it, or thought
it would go this far. How could she share him with another
woman? She had made a terrible mistake.

She told Sedick about Soemaya's decision when he came home
from work, expecting him to laugh the whole matter off. But
Sedick didn't laugh. He asked her if she was sure she wanted him
to do this.

This was her chance to call it off. All she had to do was tell him.
Sedick would sort it all out with Soemaya. But the words that came
out of her mouth were quite different. 'Don't you want children?'
she asked.

'I would love to have children. I'm just thinking of you. How
you're going to feel.'

'So you're all right with the idea?'

'If you want me to do it.'

'You're not arguing against it. We're talking about you sleeping
with another woman.'

'Do you want me to say no?'

It wasn't quite what she wanted to hear. But it was too late
already. He hadn't rejected the idea. 'You'll be fair, won't you?' she
heard herself saying.

'Of course I'll be fair.'
'Because God says if you can't be fair you must only have one.'

On a cold Sunday morning in June, Nadia stood with her mother, Aisha, in Soemaya's mother's house and watched her husband marry her best friend. Everyone was surprised by her handling of the affair. They had never witnessed such a thing. Usually second marriages took place without the first wife knowing anything about it. In this instance, the first wife had made the proposal to the second wife, and was present at the nikkah. The imam commended her.

But Nadia felt deeply betrayed. How could her friend have done such a thing? And how could her husband go through with it? For all his declarations of love, he could be with one woman as well as another.

She went with the wedding party to the new house in Crawford her husband had bought for all of them to live in. The cottage in Newlands was no longer big enough. You had to give both women the same, and two cottages were out of the question. To be fair, Sedick bought a huge double storey on Third Avenue, and identical furniture for the lower and upper floors. He took God's Words so literally, that when you stepped into the lounge on the main floor, the coffee table, the couches, the dining-room table and chairs were exactly the same as the furniture on the top floor, and in the same positions.

Nadia had already spent a week in the house with Sedick before the wedding. She had chosen the lower floor for herself.

'Don't take upstairs,' her mother, Aisha, had said. 'If you're downstairs, you're still the one in charge when someone comes to the house. You're still the boss.'

The night of the wedding was beyond anything Nadia had ever experienced, and at one point, in the middle of the night, she almost ran upstairs to tear her husband away from her friend. She couldn't get the thought of the two of them together out of her head. Was he kissing her? Was he telling her he loved her? Was he holding her the way he held her while she drifted off to sleep? What was he feeling as he entered her? She curled up, a lonely little bird, clutching her pillow in grief.

The next morning she got up early and left the house before he came downstairs. She didn't want him to see her. He would know instantly from her face that she'd cried the whole night. And she didn't want to see Soemaya. She had agreed to alternate days, and it would be her turn that day. She didn't want a turn.

Her sewing business was still at the old address and she left early, and stayed there until four. She packed up and went to visit her mother. Aisha, an attractive woman in her early fifties, was surprised to see her there so late in the day.

'How are you, my girl?' her mother asked. 'Shouldn't you be at home?'

Nadia broke down and cried.

Aisha came and sat next to her. Nadia talked her heart out. Aisha listened. She understood very well what her daughter was going through. She herself had been a first wife, although her husband had died when Nadia was still on the breast. 'You have made a mistake,' she said.

'Yes. I didn't think Soemaya would do it, and I didn't think he would. She's my best friend. How could she? Even if I'd begged her, she shouldn't have.'

Aisha looked at her, contemplating whether she should tell her daughter. With her it had also been a best friend. But why tell her something she need never know? She had only been a first wife for

six months, and after Mogamat Noor's death, the best friend had
moved with her family to England. She had kept all of that secret.
Only her mother knew.

'Mummy looked so far away right now,' Nadia said.

Aisha smiled, and stirred honey into the lemon tea she had
poured for them. 'What are you going to do?'

'I don't know. What does Mummy think?'

'What I think and what I can tell you are not the same thing.
Some women can share, and some women can't. You agreed to the
marriage. They're married already.'

'I know, and that part of it is done, but could Mummy have
been part of such an arrangement? I know Daddy died when I was
still a baby, but could Mummy have shared him?'

Aisha took a long time to reply. 'Your father was a good man.
I …'

'What?' Nadia asked when her mother couldn't get the words
out.

'The decision was made for me.'

Nadia went home, shocked by the story her mother had told her.
She believed it now. History repeated itself. Only, in her case, her
mother had had a baby, and she never would have one. That would
be the privilege of the other wife.

She arrived home and saw the white BMW in the driveway, and
found her husband downstairs in the kitchen tossing a salad. He
wasn't upstairs. That was in his favour. She stood in the doorway
and watched him for a moment. There were no sounds coming
from the top floor. When he turned to her, she saw from his face
that he felt awkward. She knew in that moment that she couldn't
leave him. But her life had changed. She couldn't yet articulate it.
Tonight he would be with her. Tomorrow he would be upstairs.

'I didn't have time to make supper,' she said.

'It's okay. I'm not very hungry. I'm just making a salad. Would you like some?'

'No, thanks.'

She sat down at the table and watched him. What should she talk about now? Ask him how his first night had been with another woman? If the sex was good? If she swallowed? Of course she didn't swallow. Soemaya didn't know anything about sex, and had just had her cherry popped.

She got up, and went to have a shower. At 9:30 she went to bed, and pretended to be asleep when he slipped in next to her. In her heart she cried. She could make no sounds in her pillow. She couldn't let him know how she felt. But he did know. From the silence in the house, the distance she kept when they were together. The closeness they'd had had slipped away with the rising of the moon, and would never return.

For several days she managed to be out of the way when Soemaya went upstairs or downstairs on her way to and from work. After a week, she came home from her sewing business, and found Soemaya waiting for her in the lounge downstairs.

Soemaya came straight to the point. 'You're avoiding me, Nadia.'

Nadia looked at her. There was nothing in Soemaya's demeanour to indicate her new status. In fact, she had a sorry look on her face. 'You're right, I am. I'm having difficulty accepting what I've done, or what I've allowed.'

Soemaya didn't say anything right away. She waited to hear if Nadia had anything more to add. There was nothing.

'I'm going to ask Sedick for a talaq.'

A talaq! Nadia looked at her, not quite believing what she'd just heard. It was what she wanted, for Soemaya to go away and leave them alone, but Soemaya's readiness to be divorced stirred up something else in her.

'Why?'

'We've been friends a long time. I didn't know it would cause you so much pain. I prefer to be your friend.'

The words touched her. This was her friend. This was why they were friends. 'People will talk.'

'I'm not worried about the people. I want us to be the way we were. I'll talk to Sedick tonight, and I'll go home to my mother. It's in the beginning, we can still do it.'

Nadia came towards her, and they embraced. For a long time no one said anything.

'Don't talk to Sedick,' Nadia said, releasing herself. 'Give me some time to get used to this. You're sharing my husband, Soemaya – not a loaf of bread. I've had him to myself for eight years.'

'I can leave, Nadia. I'm prepared to.'

'I know you are, and thank you for that. I also want to be your friend. Just leave things as they are for the moment. None of this is your fault.'

The matter was never raised again. Nadia no longer avoided Soemaya, and Sedick never got to know how close he came to losing his second wife. Life downstairs didn't change overnight, but slowly Nadia learned to ignore the laughter and noises upstairs. She and Soemaya were best friends. Their husband was home at night. If he wasn't upstairs, he was downstairs. In time all of them went shopping together, and watched movies, and the wife whose turn it was would invite the other wife to come and have supper with them.

One night, in bed, Nadia asked the question that had been burning inside her for six months. 'Do you love her?'

Sedick buried his face in her hair. 'You're my first wife ... no one can replace you.'

They weren't exactly the words she wanted to hear, but they were enough. Her love for Soemaya had made it easier. On the one hand, she wanted to be the only one, but on the other, she also didn't want Soemaya to be someone else's second best.

A week before Ramadan, Soemaya came to have tea with her downstairs. 'I want you to be the first to know, Nadia. I don't know if it's good news for you, or bad news. I'm pregnant.'

Nadia grabbed hold of her and they hugged. 'Of course it's good news! Does Sedick know?'

'Not yet. I wanted you to be the first.' Soemaya looked at her closely. 'This will be your baby also, Nadia. He will have two mothers.'

Nadia's eyes misted up. 'You mean it?'

'I mean it. He's part of Sedick. You must be part of him.'

In bed by herself that night, Nadia thought of Soemaya and her good news. It wasn't, of course, as it would have been if Soemaya had been married to someone else and come and told her she was pregnant. She was happy for Soemaya, but there was also some longing involved: she wished it had been her, that she was the one who had come home and told her husband that they would have a child. But there was no jealousy. No anger. And she believed Soemaya when she said that the baby would have two mothers. She knew it wasn't meant literally – it couldn't be – but she also knew what it meant.

As the months passed, Soemaya shared all her experiences with her. Nadia went with her to the doctor. She was there for the blood and urine tests. She was in the waiting room when Soemaya came out and told her the even more wonderful news – that the doctor

had picked up two heartbeats. Soemaya was scheduled for an ultrasound the following week, but didn't want the doctor to tell her
the sexes of the infants.

When Sedick came home at night, there were two women
waiting for him. He had to listen to their plans, drive them to the
carpenter who was making the cribs. They didn't want those new-
looking things but old-fashioned wooden ones that rocked. The
names would be hand-carved on the headboards once they knew
the sexes of the children. Sara and Tamara, for girls. Luqman and
Hud, for boys. Soemaya's sister, Yasmina, was an artist and was
going to paint flowers and meadows on the nursery wall. Nadia
was going to crochet the jackets and bonnets and bootees and
shawls. Soemaya's mother was going to give them the baby clothes.
All Soemaya had to do was give birth.

At the same time as all this was happening, Nadia started to
become tired. She would go to her sewing business in the mornings, and return at two in the afternoon to lie on the couch. It was
common for her to have an irregular period, and she didn't go to
Dr Cohen when she didn't have one for two months. There was no
morning sickness, no bloating, no sore breasts. She put her fatigue
down to the excitement of the imminent arrival of the twins. After
three months of vitamin supplements and feeling even more tired,
she decided to go to see Dr Cohen.

The doctor examined her. 'Well, Nadia, let me tell you what has
happened to you. This happens from time to time. First, you are
very low on iron. We have to rectify this immediately. But you are,
I would say, about six months pregnant.'

'What?' She looked down at herself, putting her hand on her
belly. 'Me?'

The doctor smiled. 'Yes. Didn't you feel anything?'

Nadia was still trying to accept what she'd been told. 'No. I just felt tired. And didn't open myself up to anything. I couldn't handle another disappointment. And I purposely didn't come and see you when I missed my period. I just told myself that it was because I was excited for my friend's babies. She's expecting twins. She's married to my husband.'

'Oh.'

Nadia saw her confusion. 'It's too long to explain. But I can't believe what you've told me. And I've put on no weight – well, just a little. I felt my pants were a little tight, but not much.'

'It was perhaps better that it happened this way, that you didn't know. Except for the iron, of course. Women need lots of iron when they're pregnant.' She looked down at the date on her calendar. 'You have to come back in two weeks.'

Nadia drove straight from the doctor's office to her mother's house. Her mother hugged her when she heard the news, and they sat and had tea. 'This is a gift from God. God loves you.'

'I know.'

'Have you told Sedick yet?'

'No. I came straight here. I won't tell him now. Soemaya's due any day.'

Soemaya's water broke on the same day that Nadia had her ultrasound done. She helped Soemaya to the toilet, then called Sedick where he was at a friend's house. 'You have to come home. Soemaya has to go to hospital.'

'She's in labour?' he asked.

'Yes. Her things are all ready. You just have to come and get her.'

'I want you to come with,' Soemaya said from the couch, both hands cupping her belly after a particularly painful contraction.

'Sedick will be there with you. And your mother and sister.

Someone has to look after the house. But I will pray that everything goes well. Sedick must call me the moment it happens. It doesn't matter if it's late.'

'Why don't you want to come?'

'I told you.'

When the car was gone, Nadia took a leisurely shower and examined herself in front of the long bathroom mirror. Satisfied with her appearance, she put on her prayer robe, made salaah, and went to sleep.

At 4:30 in the morning, the phone by her bed rang. 'It's two girls, Nadia. They're beautiful!'

Nadia's eyes closed in relief. She listened to her husband for a few minutes, then said goodbye. But she didn't go back to sleep. She took a brown envelope out of her drawer, walked upstairs, through Soemaya's lounge, to the nursery next to the bedroom. She went to stand between the cribs and rocked them gently. Sara and Tamara. The names could be carved on the cribs now. She looked at the wall – a green meadow with flowers and toadstools and a giant boot with children spilling out of it. She sat down in the rocking chair and opened the envelope to look one more time at the ultrasound picture. She would tell them soon. Now it was Soemaya's turn. But soon she would tell them she was having a boy.

Number nineteen

Leaning against the bumper of his car, jingling the change in his pockets, the housing rep watched a potential customer materialise between two shacks, striding towards him. The morning was a warm one for August, the dankness rising off the township in a head of steam, exposing the glitter and gloom of dead fires, zinc shacks, scrap metal, and stripped cars propped up on bricks like old queens holding court. The rep had been there an hour already and was considering leaving for Crossroads, where he was better known, but it looked like he might have business after all. He tugged the front of his shirt, resetting his Raybans. The Raybans were real, the mark of success; the jeans and sneakers, Makro issue.

Oliver walked slowly. He recognised the housing rep from the description Moses had given. *The coloured with the yellow Ford, you can't miss him. Looks like that Johnny Mathis guy who pulls his mouth when he sings. Wears Raybans.*

Oliver was nervous. Moses Maphosa had done it. Nothing had happened. Neither the ANC nor the Nats wanted to take action and be seen as the bad guys and lose votes in the forthcoming elections. It didn't matter to Oliver. If this was part of the new leniency when the ANC took over, he was all for it. He and Lulu wanted a house with brick walls and electricity and didn't care what they had to do to get it. They couldn't take living in Khayelitsha any more.

'Molo.'

'Molo. Kunjani?'

'Are you the housing rep?' Oliver asked.

'The man with the keys,' the rep responded.

'I'm looking for a place.'

'I got one in Tafelsig.'

'How much?'

'Twelve hundred.'

'Twelve hundred rand for a council home?'

'It's got a toilet, water, 'lectricity.'

'No one's in it?'

'No one.'

Oliver hesitated. 'I got six hundred.'

The housing rep stuck his finger in the side of his mouth and dislodged a piece of breakfast. 'Can't do it,' he said. 'Overhead.'

Oliver looked at the run-down Ford with the yellow hood. 'How much?'

'I told you, twelve.'

'Seven.'

'Twelve.'

'Eight and a half.'

'Eleven.'

'Nine.'

'A thousand rand, and that's final.'

Oliver could see that negotiation was at an end. He reached into his trouser pocket and brought out a stack of R50 notes. He counted out a thousand rand, recounted it, and gave it to the rep. The rep gave him the key and address.

'Get there today.'

Oliver looked at the key in his hand. A key to a new beginning. 'What if they've moved in already?'

'They're only supposed to in two days.'

At noon the minibus taxi they'd hired arrived, and Oliver, his wife Lulu, and the twins — their Primus stove, mattress, transistor radio, planks, pots and pans and clothes stacked to the roof of the Nissan 12-seater — got their first look at their new residence. Oliver had to pay twelve fares. The house was 30 square metres, with an asbestos roof and a patch of sand in the front, annexed to another of the same colour and dimensions, one in several rows of new council homes.

'Look at that!' Lulu said. 'There's a sheet in the window!'

'It must be a mistake,' Oliver said, trying not to show his alarm. 'There's no number on the door, it can't be the house.'

'It is. The one next to it is 17. This is it, number 19. What will we do, Oliver? There're people in the house.'

The driver turned his head to look at them in the back. He had lost money already waiting for them to load up the taxi, and even though he'd charged them twelve fares, now that he knew what was happening, he wanted to be rid of them.

'Kom, mense, maak aan.' Come, folks, hurry up.

'Just wait a minute, please,' Oliver said. He got out of the van and crossed the patch of sand to the front door. He held his ear to it and knocked. He beckoned to his wife. Lulu got out of the taxi and joined him.

'That bastard ripped us off,' Oliver said. 'Fucking coloured!'

Lulu looked at him. 'And now?'

'We're going in.'

Lulu looked nervously about her. 'I'm scared, Oliver. Someone else lives here. How can we move in? Their things are in the house. They'll come home.'

Oliver took out the key and slid it into the lock. It opened easily, and they stood on the doorstep, looking into a small lounge with a brushed nylon settee, a thin-legged coffee table and a television set on a Pepsi-Cola crate. The house was box-like, divided in four, with a lounge, kitchen, two tiny bedrooms and a bathroom whose toilet you could see from the front door. The lounge was next to the kitchen, and a formica table with four plastic chairs was pressed up against the settee, the rest of the small space being taken up by a stove and fridge and several boxes on the floor, indicating that people had recently moved in. There were no ceilings and no plugs in the rooms except for one in the kitchen and lounge, but to Oliver and Lulu, who had never had electricity, running water or a toilet, it was luxury.

'We have to take their things out,' Oliver said.

Lulu could feel the pressure in her bladder and wanted desperately to pee. She peed very much in the cold weather and August had been a cold month. She was nervous. This wasn't what she'd expected would happen, and there was no turning back once they entered the house. She looked back at her six-year-old twins in front of the taxi, where she'd instructed them to remain: barefoot, shivering, wanting to come out of the cold. The rep had lied to them, taken their money and given them a bad key. There was no money left to make other plans, and by now their vacated shack in Khayelitsha would've been claimed by someone else.

She and Oliver entered the house and went immediately for the couch, dragging it out. The driver saw what was happening and pressed down hard on his hooter, shouting that if they didn't come right away to fetch their belongings, he would drive off with them. The girls helped Lulu unload the taxi while Oliver carried mattresses and blankets and chairs from the house, racing against time before the legal occupants arrived. An hour later, every item in the house was out on the sand patch in front. Oliver secured the pile with blankets held down in four places with bricks. Then he and Lulu and the children moved their own things into the house.

'That's it. We're in,' he sighed.

Lulu watched the door shut behind them. Surrounded by boxes and children, the silence of cement walls, the enormity of what they had done curled into her like a slow-moving serpent and settled in the pit of her stomach. From the moment Oliver had come with the key, she had been swept along by the swell of events, with no time to consider repercussions, even though they had discussed doing what Moses had done many times. All she wanted was a house where the roof didn't leak and where there was water and toilet facilities. They hadn't only entered a property illegally, but had broken into a tenanted one. How were the people going to react when they came home and found their belongings out on the street?

'I don't know what to do,' Lulu said. 'I'm frightened. These people will be very angry. We've taken their home. They might kill us.'

'We've moved in, Lulu. Unpack. This place is ours now. Make sandwiches.'

'How can you eat at a time like this?'

'We've eaten through worse times.'

There was little conversation as they went about unpacking their things, and took turns at the window guarding the goods of the occupants whose worldly possessions they had deposited out on the sand patch in front of the house. Towards evening Oliver went outside to threaten a youth fingering the television set and resettled the blankets and bricks to keep everything safe and in place. When he came back in, he found Lulu sniffling into her sleeve.

'What's wrong?' he asked.

'These people have children. Where will they go?'

'You can't feel sorry for them. We have children also. Who's sorry for us?'

'What if they have a gun?'

'They don't have a gun.'

'But what if they do?'

'It's too late to cry now, Lulu. We have to go through with it. We gave that skelm the last of our money. He said there was no one in the house. He lied to us. What choice do we have?'

'They could bring the police.'

'We have to take a chance like Moses did and hope nothing happens to us.'

At 6:15, a VW Microbus with the logo I'M TOO SEXY FOR MY TEXI painted in bold letters on the side of the van screeched to a halt outside the door. Oliver and Lulu watched from the window as the people whose house they had invaded emerged from the van, shocked to find their belongings out on the street. The woman got out first, nervously examining the goods under the blanket, then turned to her husband, who was too stunned to believe he was standing in front of his own house. The taxi drove off, leaving a jet of exhaust fumes swirling about them, and the man and woman looked at the intruders staring at them through the window. Then something snapped in the woman and she ran screaming to the front door, banging on it with her shoe.

'Open the door!' she yelled. 'Errol, don't stand there! Call the police!'

A crowd of people gathered in the street. They'd known all day that something was going to happen. A dozen houses had been invaded in the past few weeks. No police vans had arrived, nothing had been done. No one wanted to touch the Tafelsig fiasco. The people had to sort themselves out until it was decided just who would give the eviction order. The outgoing government was sitting back, enjoying the chaos. The ANC, afraid of losing black votes in the forthcoming elections, turned a blind eye.

Oliver and his family watched the husband come up and say something to his wife still banging on the door.

'I don't care!' the wife shouted. 'This is our house! We gave money to move in! We waited five years for a house, I'm not going! Kom uit, julle donders!'

Inside the house, Lulu leaned against the wall, charged with fear. She realised that the people making a commotion outside the door were themselves not the legal occupants. They, too, had paid someone for a key.

'Did you hear that, Oliver? They also paid for a key.'

'We can't help that.'

The screaming and banging continued and Oliver covered the windows with blankets and moved a chair under the knobs of the front and back doors.

'Go in there with the children,' he ordered her.

It was dark in the bedroom, but Lulu didn't switch on the light. A crash behind her made her jump and she ran back out to the lounge. A brick had come hurtling through the window, and lay in a bed of splintered glass on the cement floor. Oliver directed her with his eyes to go back in the room, then picked up a thick piece of wooden shelving that he'd brought along. When he thought the woman was directly behind the door, he slammed into it with brute force. There was a moment's silence, then a barrage of profanity and a terrifying volley of shattering glass as windows shivered and exploded all around them.

In the bedroom Lulu listened to the noise, her children trembling before her. She couldn't let them see how she felt. They'd seen enough in their six years. She was through with peeing outside in the cold, tired of the buckets and bowls dotted about the cardboard floor catching dripping water, tired of the constant danger. When their shack had been set alight, they had escaped with R8 in Oliver's pocket, watching their belongings go up in smoke. The neighbours knew who it was, but valued their own safety: community worked for you, but also against you. Moses, still in Khayelitsha, took them in. When Moses invaded the house in Tafelsig, she and Oliver inherited his shack. Still, what they'd just done put them in the same league as those criminals they wanted to get away from, and presented a different anxiety. Tafelsig was coloured territory. Coloureds didn't like blacks. The night might find them jailed or dead.

Outside the door the banging and shouting was still going on, but slowly losing velocity like a dog who'd barked itself out, giving a few for-appearances'-sake growls at the end. Lulu rummaged in the box at her feet and found clean clothes for her children. She took them into the bathroom and poured water into the small plastic bath. The water was cold, but she would heat the kettle on the Primus stove and give them a real bath. Like other people. People who lived in real houses with real bathrooms and bathed their children in foamy water. She had a real house now. Her children didn't have to stand with their bums in the wind and feel a cold rag down their backs.

As if in a dream, she went to the kitchen and filled the kettle and pumped the Primus stove, ignoring the broken bricks and glass on the floor. The water boiled quickly and she took the kettle into the bathroom and poured it into the plastic tub, whipping up dish-detergent bubbles with her hand. The bath could barely hold two, and she washed their faces and necks, then had them sit in the thick foam. The pleasure of the hot water and lather on their skins, all the more pleasurable because of their mother's attendance, made the girls drowsy. When they'd had enough, Lulu dressed them in warm clothes and sat with them on her lap above the pile of dirty clothes on the floor. She stayed with them in the dark until their heads crushed her bosom in sleep and Oliver came finally to tell her that it was over.

'A van came for their things. They're gone.'

Lulu couldn't believe it. How could you lose your home like this in a day and accept it? 'They're gone? Their things also?'

'Yes. Go to bed. I'll sit up just in case they come back.'

Lulu went to bed with the children, and Oliver stuffed newspaper into the broken windows. No one slept. Not that night, and not the night after. Oliver stayed home three days from work and changed the locks. He watched from the window, waiting for something to happen. No policemen arrived, no one from the council showed up at their door. There was no sign of the people whose belongings they had put out on the street.

The weeks passed. Oliver and Lulu went quietly on with their lives. They met the neighbours and came to know the beat of the neighbourhood. It wasn't so bad living amongst coloureds. They shared the same grievances, and were all waiting for the new government to come in and make good on campaign promises. To their left lived a man who fixed cars with stolen parts. To their right was a Hadji selling koeksisters to cafés and schools. At the back an unmarried teacher resided with a teenage daughter. Across the road was a shebeen run by a feisty old woman called Ouma Ball, who could drink any customer under the table.

Lulu became friends with the Hadji, who gave her a job frying and sugaring the coconut-covered doughnuts, and in no time she was earning enough money to buy clothes for her children and help contribute towards the food.

Ten days before Christmas, there was a knock on the door. Oliver went to open it. 'Moses! What a surprise …' He looked over Moses's shoulder at the van parked in front of his house, loaded with mattresses and tables and chairs.

'Olivah, Olivah. The worst thing has happened. The sheriff came at five this morning when we were all asleep. I don't believe it, my friend. Everything was going so nicely. Somebody wake up and say, hey, go throw Moses out in the street. I was wondering, man, we have no place. It's just Mary and me and the kids. Do you have some place for us to sleep?'

Postcards from South Africa

The small house sat boxed between a shebeen and a double-storey structure on Gympie Street. It was after sunset, the roads cleansed of the fuss of the day, Sunday night. Sunday nights was when he came. After a Sea Point lunch and outing with his young, second wife.

Munieba stared at her face in the bathroom mirror. She didn't care that he came only one night a week. It saved her from having to do a lot of things. Things for which she no longer had any feeling.

She smoothed some cream into her neck, brushed her teeth, and put on her scarf. She checked her wristwatch for the time, and went into the front room to sit with her mother, who was watching a documentary on television.

The doorbell rang and she let him in. Hamid sat for a few minutes with her and her mother in the lounge, accepting a cup of tea, which Munieba set in front of him with a few biscuits.

Afterwards, they went to her room. In the room, he sat on the bed with the duvet with the ANC colours he'd bought her for her 55th birthday a year ago. The colours worked for the flag, but not for a duvet. It was too harsh for the softness of her room. The duvet came out only on Sundays. The rest of the time she slept under white lace covers, where the smells and fragrances were her own.

'How're you?' he asked.

'Okay.'

He took off his trousers. She took them from him and hung them up. A clean shirt, pressed for the next day, with socks and underwear, were on the chair, ready for the next morning when he would get up at 6:30, have a shower, and go to his service station in Rylands. She wouldn't see him again until the following Sunday. When it was her turn. One night out of seven.

'I see *Asoka* is showing at Cavendish Square.' She wasn't Indian but had always gone to see all the Indian movies with him.

He pulled back the duvet and got into bed.

'Shariefa wants to go.'

She said nothing. She had long ago given up thinking about Shariefa. Second wives got it all. Shariefa got six nights, a new Mercedes, a mansion on Sandown Road with high walls and security. She was back in her mother's humble little house. She got R500 for groceries.

She thought of her friends, Fatima and Mariam. They'd both had disappointments. But for them life was a merry-go-round of eat 'n' treat functions, spooning trifle into their mouths as they watched the passing parade.

'We can go to a movie on Wednesday night,' he said, when she didn't respond. 'I'll come early.'

She removed her scarf, and hung it neatly over the back of a chair. He looked at her for a moment.

'You've changed the colour of your hair. It looks red.'

'I put henna on it. It just looks redder in this candlelight.'

He nodded. 'It looks nice.'

She gave a wan smile. How long was she going to wait, she wondered. What was she afraid of? The loneliness? What people would say? She went shopping and to family functions by herself. She was alone. What was stopping her? She didn't need his R500. She had a good job as a receptionist at a clothing factory in Salt River. She'd always had a good voice. She had friends. And she was still an attractive woman. She didn't have to be like her friends. Fatima and Mariam were comfortable in their robes, and the extra weight they carried around their middles. Not her. She didn't eat pies or samoosas. She walked home in her walking shoes after work. She never ate potatoes. And she included lots of vegetables and fruit in her diet.

'What did you do last night? he asked.

'What I do every Saturday night. I watch a movie and fall asleep on the couch.'

He was quiet for a moment. 'You know I can't change things.'

She stepped out of her slip, holding in her stomach until she was under the covers.

He pulled her towards him.

She allowed his hands on her body. 'Hamid?'

He stopped. 'Am I hurting you?' he asked.

The glow of the candlelight on her face made her look like a young woman. 'I want a talaq.'

The buildings were long, brown-bricked, austere. Sam looked at the guards up ahead at the gate, the emerald lawns, the wire fence. What had come first, she wondered, the incongruous prison or the stately homes? Pollsmoor was smack in the middle of the exclusive neighbourhood of Tokai.

'Do you have any weapons?' one of the guards asked, peering into the car.

'No.'

'What's your business?'

'I'm an attorney. Here to see a prisoner.'

She signed in. He let her through.

At the main building she went to the second floor, filled in a permit for a legal visit at the desk at the top of the stairs and waited at the window, where she studied the blue aluminium window frames with their narrow strips of glass. She looked around for a moment at the posters in three languages. *Stop Abortions. Unborn South Africans have the right to live. AKUTSHAYWA. MOENIE ROOK NIE.* The place was a hive of activity, with guards and lawyers and visitors waiting for prisoners to be brought to interview rooms.

A black woman enquired after a brother. 'No, Mama, down there. Yes, Mama, he's in a different block.' The new South Africa. Friendly, coloured, black. Inmates with good behaviour cajoled the guards, got light duty, privileges. Behind the steel doors and bars, they sat around in groups playing cards, 40 and 50 to a cell: rapists and murderers thrown in with juvenile delinquents and petty thieves. The guards wore brown pants and jerseys with a leather strap over the shoulder ending in the trouser pocket, holding a ring of keys. No guns. Only a baton down the side of the leg.

The prisoner arrived. He was short, with a diamond in one of his front teeth, the words 'God forgives. I don't' tattooed like a choker round his neck. She wondered whose ring the diamond had come from, what hand, and whether the hand was still attached to the body, or rotting in a park or on a deserted beach somewhere. She'd seen a hand chopped off with a panga, found by the police in a Cape Flats subway. Red nails at one end, maggots at the other.

The guard escorted them to a large room with blank walls, a pool of sun spilling through the grilled windows onto the interview tables.

'You're a woman,' he said suddenly. 'I didn't know they were sending me a woman.'

'Do you know why I'm here?'

'To defen' me.'

'You're charged with carjacking and three counts of robbery and assault. Do you want to tell me what happened?'

'I told the police I never touch that car. I was waiting for someone when it happened. A gun went off.'

'It was your gun.'

'Lady, lookit.' He pulled open the collar on his shirt, exposing the keloid scars of three bullet holes. 'This one here just miss the vein. I carry a gun, yes, I live in Valhalla Park. You know Valhalla Park, lady? I don't think you know. White people don't know these things. They only know defendants. In Valhalla Park they murder you in your own house while you sleep. The holes in the car's not from me, I promise you. The robberies I did. I'm not ashamed to say I did it.'

'Why?'

The diamond flashed. 'They lay me off before Krismas. I got six kids. How must I feed them?'

'You stuck a knife in a woman's back.'

'I wanted her money, not her life. People depen' on me to eat. When you don't have money, you do anything. I have a aambag, lady, I'm a boilermaker. Yes, a boilermaker. You look at me and you think I'm a gangster. I'm not. I have a trade. But they lay me off and I have nothing to give to my family. My children don't even have shoes. I go to the union. They don't wanna hear my story, they have a hundred stories. This is the new South Africa. A coloured can't get into the navy with matric, but blacks get in with Stanerd Five! I'm a ANC man, lady, I voted for Mandela, but tell me affirmative action's not for the blacks. When the whites ruled, I couldn't go anywhere, but I had money because I had work. Now I can go everywhere, but I have no money. Whatsa use? The President's dancing so much on TV, he forgot about us. We still in the middle. Yes, lady, I rob and I steal, and I do it again if I come out and have no work.'

George stood on the pavement in front of Cape Town station and looked around for a taxi that would take him the short ride to Sea Point. Gone were the separate queues, buses to Sea Point, cabs for whites. The minibus taxi was the new dog on the road. Cheap, fast and overcrowded, it bullied its way through traffic, made unexpected stops, jumped lanes without indicating, and frequently got into violent skirmishes with other taxis and motorists. He'd once been in a friend's car when a taxi with a sticker on its side saying GIVE WAY CAUSE I WON'T A DAMN GIVE WAY FOR YOU snaked out from behind, jumped the kerb, and cut in right in front of them at the light. The ticket collector leaned out the window and gave them the finger and swore at them for not getting out of the way fast enough.

How had the country slid into such disrespect and senseless violence, he wondered. And how had his life changed so drastically that he was reduced to travelling in a taxi, and living in a basement apartment smaller than the stable in which he'd kept his lambing ewes? A decade ago he was a sheep farmer with 4000 hectares of land, running a posse of blacks. Today, he had R13 in his pocket. The cars, land, livestock, house, all that was sucked up and gone. Smuggling Krugerrands into the United States had been the beginning of a series of losses, including his wife to a surfer in Malibu. Returning to South Africa, he lost the rest of his money in bad investments. He was lucky to find a job in agriculture. It was work he liked, the pay was good, the atmosphere friendly. Then the bad news. Contracts were drying up, they were cutting down. Last in were first to go.

He turned at the rush of commuters barrelling out of the station. The area was crowded with street vendors hawking their wares. He was hungry, in the mood for a steak and kidney pie, but couldn't afford the R3. His fridge was empty. He needed milk, bread, something to put on the bread. He had to hang onto the change in his pocket. Tomorrow he would visit Dennis on Albany Road and borrow R200 to tide him over until he found work. He had helped Dennis in the past. Dennis would reciprocate.

'Bo-Kaap!' a young boy shouted, leaning out of the passenger window of a white mini-van. George wondered if they were going further on.

'Can you swing by Sea Point?' he asked.

The boy looked at him, then turned to the driver, a big black with a surly expression.

'We not going that way, we going to Bo-Kaap, but okay, get in. R1.50.'

George fished the change out of his pocket, and handed it to him.

'Molo.'

'Molo,' the driver rolled his eyes.

George smiled. He could read the driver's thoughts. Another whitey with two words of Xhosa in his repertoire. It was fashionable to show a black you could speak his language, a prerequisite now for many jobs. 'Can't speak Xhosa? Sorry, we need someone who can speak the language.' A safe rejection for wrong-skinned applicants.

The taxi was headed for the Bo-Kaap, also known as the Malay Quarter, and he pressed in next to a woman in the back row eating a packet of chips. The smell of the vinegar on the hot chips was more than he could bear, and if the woman had turned to him even once he would've asked if he could have one.

The taxi zipped up through the business section of Wale Street, all the way to the top, where office buildings abruptly changed to spice shops and tailors and mosques and quaint flat-roofed, Moorish houses with fanlights and heavy oak doors – some white-washed and restored – built in the 18th century by the Cape slaves. The driver took a right on Chiappini Street for two young women who wanted to get out, a left on Longmarket Street for the lady with the chips, and stopped in front of a mosque on the next road where the last of the passengers got out. They continued on to Strand Street, turned left, and lumbered up the hill into Sea Point.

George moved up behind the driver and the fare collector.

'How's business in the taxi trade?' he asked.

The driver looked at him in the rearview mirror.

'Where'd you learn to speak Xhosa like that?'

'I grew up on a farm in the Eastern Cape. We had a lot of blacks working for us.'

The driver had a matchstick between his lips and moved it around from left to right. His passenger was blue-jeaned, with leather boots and a cowboy hat, and reminded him of those husky men in American cigarette ads. Not the kind he saw getting into his taxi every day.

'I'm also from up there.'

'Really?'

'Couldn't take the drought. Came down here. More opportunity in the Cape. The taxi business? Not bad if you can persuade the bank to give you money to get one of these.'

'How much?'

The driver smacked his hand on the dashboard. 'A minibus, this model, R40 000, second-hand.'

'That's a lot of fares.'

'And a lot of headaches. People think that when you drive a

taxi, you're rich. There're payments to banks, insurance companies, you have to buy parts, service the van, and there're so many of us on the road now, sometimes we stand half an hour without moving. Also, with petrol going up, it's getting worse.'

'It must be a dangerous job. The papers are full of stories. People shooting each other over fares and territories.'

'Yah. Those ones make all of us look bad. But we're not all road jockeys. A lot of drivers don't have their own vehicles, they rent. That's where the problem starts, why there're so many accidents. They're inexperienced, in it just to make money till they can find regular work. They don't care how they drive, if they damage the vehicles. They have accidents and disappear, leaving the owners to face the insurance companies. What line are you in now?'

'Nothing at the moment.'

'Retired?'

'No. I sold my farm in Queenstown ten years ago and went to America. It didn't work out.'

'You didn't like it?'

'Not as an illegal immigrant.'

The driver turned around to look at him.

'You were an illegal?'

'Yes. You need a green card to become a resident. That's harder to get than an appointment with the President. The money that was supposed to make our application look good was lost on bad advice from a friend. We were rejected, but stayed on. Three years in the States without work, you spend money. It ate into the reserves. To keep us going, I drove trucks across state. I got caught working without a permit.'

'That's too bad.'

'I came back here and put what was left into a business, hired a manager. The manager cooked the books and deposited most of the money into his own account. You can do the maths. After that, I got regular work and taught agricultural farming for four years. In July the college had their own troubles. They called me in and gave me the speech. I've been looking for work ever since.'

The driver nodded sympathetically. 'So it happens to you, too.'

'More than you know.'

'You speak Xhosa. That should help.'

George laughed, surprised at the ease with which he had opened up to this stranger. 'They want younger, hungrier. People of colour. I'm a farmer, don't forget. Who's going to hire a white man of 55 with no skills?'

They were on High Level Road, overlooking the sea and the city.

'We're in Sea Point,' the driver said. 'Where do you want to go?'

'Drop me off at the top of Ocean View.'

The driver took a left and went up the steep incline and followed the road all the way across Sea Point to Fresnaye. He whistled as they passed some of the millionaire mansions on the mountainside.

'You live in a fine area.'

'In a basement. I have a room and a toilet. Here's fine, you can stop at the corner coming up.'

The driver stopped the van and turned around to look at George as he was getting out the side door. 'Listen ...' he said, holding out his hand. 'Keep this.'

George looked at the R1.50 he had paid the fare collector earlier. Could he take it? He looked at the driver. There was no pity in his eyes, just a heavy-lidded look that said he had to be on his way.

George hesitated only seconds. 'Thanks, man,' he said. 'I appreciate it.'

Brenda came out of a deep sleep and listened for a moment to the soft snore of her youngest daughter, Melinda, next to her in bed. She'd heard a noise, scratchy and persistent. Was it in the house? At the door? She got up quietly and slipped on her gown. The digital clock glowed 2:45 in the dark. She had lifted Melinda to carry her to her bed in the next room when she heard it again. She put Melinda back down on the bed and ran to the window and looked out. Parked in the street in front of his house was old Pa Visagie's white Passat. Leaning into the passenger side of the car was a man pulling at something inside.

She ran to the phone and dialled Pa Visagie's number. The old man answered almost immediately.

'Pa ...' she said quickly into the mouthpiece. 'It's Brenda. From opposite. I know it's late, but there's someone stealing your car radio.'

'I know,' he whispered.

'You know?'

'Yes. I'm watching him ten minutes now.'

'Have you called the police?'

'No.'

'Why not?'

'Let him maar take the radio. It's safer.'

'Pa, you're whispering. He can't hear you.'

'Am I whispering?'

'Yes.'

'I'm going to call the police.'

'No.'

'Yes, Pa.'

She hung up, but didn't call. The police would arrive when the thief was long gone. Still, she couldn't just stand there and do nothing. Pa Visagie was a pensioner, his pleasures limited to church and his hothouse tomatoes lined up like stately maidens in clay pots in the stuffy little lean-to in the yard. There was no money for extras, or another radio, and she was sure he wasn't insured. But Pa Visagie, like most people, had adopted the fear. The new government was soft on crime. Young offenders were set free. Rapists got bail. The death penalty had been scrapped. If you reported someone to the police, you feared revenge.

She didn't have a gun like some of her neighbours and wished she had something to go outside and confront the thief with. She remembered the cricket bat in Melinda's room. Melinda wouldn't sleep by herself because of a school friend who'd been abducted from her own house while her parents were having breakfast in the kitchen, and Brenda usually transferred her to her room when she was asleep.

She fetched the bat from the next room and headed for the front door. Snapping on the lights, she charged out in her voluminous gown, hurling the bat through the air.

The thief heard the commotion behind him and turned. The bat missed his head by inches and landed on top of the car with a thunk. Spotlighted where he stood and alarmed by the woman snorting towards him like a wildebeest, he dropped the radio and ran.

'You bastard coward!' she shouted after him. 'You come back here and I'll shoot!'

The thief ran on and in seconds was swallowed up by the night.

'Jesus, Brenda, that was a stupid thing to do.' Ouma Mostert materialised out of the dark. She had been standing on her stoep the whole time. 'He could've had a gun.'

'That's right,' Mervin Jenkins agreed, crossing the road in his slippers to come and stand at the gate. He, too, had witnessed everything from his veranda. 'That's the third car broken into this month. I don't know why old man Visagie doesn't park his car in the garage. Can all those flower pots and junk he keeps in there be more important than his car?'

'He's a stubborn old man,' Ouma Mostert said. 'It's sad what's happening to this country. They keep promising they going to put an end to the crime, but it's all talk. You can say what you want about the Nats, it was better under them.'

Brenda looked at the house opposite. The lace curtain moved, but Pa Visagie, his wife or spinster daughter remained put. No lights came on. She looked at Ouma Mostert and nodded. It was pointless arguing with the old lady. Ouma Mostert was one of those fair-skinned coloureds who believed all the nonsense fed to them by the suddenly conscience-stricken National Party and its propaganda machine.

'Well, let's hope that's the end of it,' she said. 'Lock your door, Ouma. You too, Mr Jenkins.' She went to the car, picked up the radio and tape deck that the thief had dropped and put it on the floor on the passenger's side and locked the door. Back in her house she heated a glass of milk and sat on a stool at her bedroom window. She would keep watch for a while. At breakfast she would tell Melinda what had happened because Melinda would hear about it from other children.

For a long time she sat sipping her milk at the window. Eventually she crawled into bed and went to sleep. In the morning, when she went to the front door to fetch the *Cape Times* the paper boy delivered at seven o'clock, she saw a fancy basket filled to the brim with shiny, bright red tomatoes.

Tokyo Mosheusheu was in a buoyant mood as he came cruising over the bridge and stopped for the red lights in front of the Lansdowne Police Station. It was nine o'clock in the morning. He'd already collected the samoosa money from two shopkeepers on his

Athlone round. He only had two more stops before delivering the van and the money to Zenosha Foods and hopping on the noon bus for the Transkei, where he would spend the Christmas holidays with his family. He hadn't seen his mother and sisters in a year and was looking forward to it.

The robot lights changed, he moved into first gear, and at the same time the door on his left was yanked open and he looked into the face of an angry youth pointing a snub-nosed gun at his head.

'Drive!'

Tokyo's heart pummelled against his chest. He changed gears and moved the van evenly into the traffic. It had happened right in front of the police station. It was a fearless bastard who would pull something like this 50 yards from the front door of the law. The name Sindile was painted in black letters on a white T-shirt. There were no whites or coloureds called Sindile. Sindile was black like he was. Stupid as well as fearless.

'Take the money, man!' he said without regard for whose money it was. 'I got R300, take it! Take everything and let me go!'

Sindile was sitting sideways on the seat with the gun jammed in Tokyo's waist. He looked at the trays of samoosas in the back of the van, reached over with his right hand and grabbed a handful, stuffing the spicy, meat-filled triangles into his mouth.

'Give me the money.'

Tokyo pulled a small black bag from under the front of his seat and handed it over.

'It's all there. I got nothing else. Just take it, and let me go. I swear I won't do anything. Just let me go. It's my last day, man, I'm leaving for the Transkei to go see my mother.'

'Shut up!' The hijacker opened the bag with one hand, letting the tens and twenties spill onto his lap. He stuffed the cash into an inside pocket, and threw the bag into the back of the van.

'Get onto the M5, and keep going.'

Tokyo looked at him sideways. They were practically the same age. Why was he doing this? Where was he taking him? He turned the van around and headed for the highway.

'Where we going, man? I gave you the money. Just let me out.'

Sindile nudged the gun deeper into his ribs.

Tokyo exited onto the highway and looked longingly at the other vehicles passing him by. What was going to happen to him? In an hour the Indian woman he worked for was going to start worrying, aware of his plans to leave for the Transkei at noon. Probably she would think he was making off with the van and the money. He felt helpless. He couldn't call out or make signs to any of the passing motorists.

'Stay in the right-hand lane, and go onto the N2.'

Tokyo felt a fluttering in his chest. They were leaving the city. What had he done to deserve this? How could one black do this to another? But it happened every day. In the township, at the taxi rank, on the train. Was the hijacker going to kill him and dump his body on the national road? He was crazy enough. The needle on the petrol gauge showed they were on empty. His face felt wet. He realised he was crying.

'Don't waste your tears, man. Your life's worth shit.'

'Why're you doing this, Sindile? I gave you the money — '

'Don't call me Sindile.'

'Just let me out, man. I want to go home. My mother's waiting for me. Please, man ...' He was shaking so badly, his arm rattled the steering wheel. There was tremendous pressure in his bowels.

'Shut up or I'll shoot you in the fucking head!'

Tokyo had become suddenly angry. Sindile looked to be the same age as him. The only difference was the gun in his hand. It gave him the power. Without it, he would've taken him on. His anger mounted. If he was going to die, it would be here, in the express lane of the highway, not in some remote area. And he would take Sindile with him.

'Do it, then! I'll drive into the oncoming traffic and kill us both!'

Sindile gave him a crack on the head with the gun. Tokyo's head knocked into the side window, and he almost lost control of the van. He jammed his foot down on the accelerator and pushed the vehicle to its limit.

'Slow down!'

Tokyo went faster.

Sindile hit him again.

'Take that exit coming up. Hesitate and I'll shoot!'

Tokyo felt fresh panic. People had been raped and killed on that road. It was a secluded strip. No houses, people, only bush. He had seconds to make the exit. With the barrel of the gun pushed into his ear, he had no choice but to do as he was told. Then, without warning, the van spluttered, slowed down, and came to a halt.

'What the fuck are you stopping for?'

'We're out of petrol.'

'What?!'

'It won't go further. The tank's empty.'

It was a crucial moment. The hijacker could panic and do something rash. He was holding someone hostage in a van that wasn't going anywhere. Still, Tokyo was grateful for where the van had come to a stop. They had just cleared the exit and were on the shoulder of the road. Not out of danger, but not isolated either. If Sindile wanted to kill him, he had to shoot him right where he sat, in full view of passing motorists.

'Take off your shirt.'

'What?' It was a new denim shirt, bought specially for his trip home.

'Take it off!' Sindile repeated.

They were sitting next to each other, the gun pointed at his head. Tokyo knew it was pointless to argue. He unbuttoned the shirt and handed it over.

'The jeans, too, and the shoes.'

'No, man, please …'

Sindile shoved the gun in his face.

'Take the fucking jeans off!'

Tokyo looked out the window. A truck had just passed on his side. He undid the belt and wriggled out of the jeans and removed his shoes.

'Get out!'

'I'm naked, man.'

'You want me to fucking shoot you?'

'Just give me my jeans. That's all I ask,' Tokyo begged.

Sindile leaned over him, opened the door, and shoved him out with his foot.

Tokyo fell onto the gravel shoulder and felt the rush of wind on his naked body as a car rushed by from behind. He looked up at Sindile.

'Please, man, my jeans …'

Sindile ignored him. He had the shoes in his hand, and turned them over to inspect the soles. Then threw them out the window at Tokyo. 'You can keep these, they stink. Now get the fuck out of my sight before I shoot you.' He fired a shot in the air.

Tokyo took off with the shoes in his hand. He ran back up the incline to the highway. Filled with shame. He had lost everything. More than his clothes and the Indian woman's van and money. Who would believe it? And who would stop for him? A black man? Naked?

A mile from where the van was stranded – shivering, stammering – he cupped his hands over his privates, and started to run.

You are the daughter

Aqeena entered the room silently. It had been a sewing room until three hours ago. A room she had spent many happy hours in, listening to the comforting buzz of the old Pfaff with the treadle as her mother hummed along to a Frank Sinatra or Dean Martin tune. As a child, she would play with her dolls and crayons and colouring books near the window in the splash of sun, nibbling on biscuits or bon-bons. When she was older, her mother would sit with her on the little couch with the clutter of patterns and materials, and they would talk about husbands and children, and marriages that worked. Now it was a room of the dead. Cleared of furniture, fabrics, photographs and history, except for the metal katel placed in the middle of the room, and a small side table holding the burial cloth.

Her aunts were in the room already, listening to the toeka-mandie's instructions. They had been with Aqeena for the roggel – her mother's last breath – and were now part of the final wash.

'We don't talk about what we see in here,' the toekamandie said, 'not even with family. What we see, stays in this room.'

Aqeena stood at the head of the katel and looked down at her mother's grey hair, the ends creeping out under the sheet. Did hair straighten in death, she wondered. Her mother's had always had a wave. Now, it lay flat and metallic against stainless steel.

'Listen, my girl, it's in that cupboard over there. In the box.'

'What, Mom?'

'My kafan.'

She had looked at her mother, stunned. 'What's Mummy talking about?'

'I'm talking about my burial cloth. You mustn't be afraid of these things.'

'You're going to live a long time, Mummy, don't talk like that. It's bad luck.'

But her mother had never been afraid of anything, and had gone to the shop and bought the white winding sheet in which her body would enter the ground. 'When it happens, my girl, the toekamandie will come to you. You are the daughter. She'll ask if there's anything in the house. You must know where it is.'

The toekamandie had come. She'd asked. Aqeena had taken out the box from the bedroom cupboard. The kafan was laid out on a side table, lined with cottonwool and dried rose leaves, stitched on one side, open on the other for the body to be inserted, like a letter into an envelope. Her mother, who didn't like perfume, tight clothes and small spaces, would go sealed and scented into her grave. She would be placed in a half-sitting position, on her side, facing east. She would face Qiblah. In time her bones would blend with the earth.

'We'll start from the top,' the toekamandie said. 'Then the washing of the private parts. It's better for one of the family. Aqeena?'

Aqeena looked at the woman who'd spoken. What went through the mind of a toekamandie, she wondered. What special thing did she possess? The task of washing and dressing the dead had nothing glamorous to recommend it; only spiritual reward. Did she do it to be constantly reminded of the swiftness of life? Did toekamandies feel closer to God? She had always thought that the washers of the dead were old women, but Moena Toefy was a lively woman in her thirties who, besides reading the Qur'an, also read Toni Morrison and Leonard Wolf. Moena owned a library card, and when she wasn't at someone's house washing the dead, or filling home orders for cake, her head was bent over a book. It was said that when Moena recited from the Qur'an, the heavens opened and the angels themselves stopped to listen.

'What must I do?'

Moena handed her a pile of linen strips. 'Wrap these around your left hand. The sheet will remain on the mayyit at all times. Make sure you cover your fingers. The hand mustn't touch the private parts. Wash it three times, each time with a clean cloth. On the third wash, check to see if there's anything showing on the cloth. If there is, wash it again, ending on an uneven number.'

It was strange hearing her mother referred to as the mayyit. The mayyit had always been someone else: her grandfather, her uncle, her best friend in a drowning accident. Mothers didn't die. They were indestructible. There for ever.

'Can you do it?' Moena asked.

Aqeena's eyes filled. 'Yes.' She moved to the foot end. She, who had always been so afraid of the dead. Her tears dropped onto the sheet. She wrapped the cloths around her hand and dipped it into the warm water at her side, rubbing Sunlight soap onto it. Sunlight soap left no scent on the body. She slid her hand under the sheet.

Oh Mom, how will I go on without you? I'm so glad I told you I loved you. Some children don't get the chance, or can't say the words. You were more than a mother to me. I could tell you things. You always listened, always gave the best advice. Still, Mom, there was something I kept from you. I never told you about him. I never told you when I remembered it for the first time. Where I was, what happened to me when the memory came. I didn't want you to know. Just in case you knew who he was. Just in case he was close to you. Just in case you had to choose. I was two, Mom. In nappies still when he took me out of the cot.

She looked at her aunts working on the arms and the hands. Auntie Rukeya, only a pucker between her brows to show the gravity of her grief, her hands working expertly under the sheet. Auntie Gaya, the youngest, weeping openly. The death had been a shock. Her mother hadn't told anyone what the doctor had said that rainy July afternoon when she'd gone to check out the lump in her breast.

Remember the house on Harrow Road, Mom? The skipping ropes, the park, the pine trees on the corner where the children came after school to play? Those should've been happy days. When girls play with dolls and believe in princes who will protect them from witches and dragons and nasty men. There were many times I wanted to take you there, Mom, to tell you about me at that time. I was little, but knew already that something was wrong. I didn't know what. I didn't believe in Snow White and Goldilocks, and if I was taken in at all by fairy tales, it was always by the wickedness to the little girl.

The water dripped down from the katel through the small drain into the plastic bath positioned underneath. The slow drip, dull and heavy, drummed home the foreverness of death. It was the end. The end of worrying about the end.

He wore a hat, Mom. I remember the colour, brown, the pattern of the wallpaper in the room, blue and pink flowers, the glass he slid himself into – up and down, up and down. Afterwards, the glass is milky and clouded. But I can't see his face. It's hidden from me. I don't know why I can't see it. Sometimes I reach back to see if some small thing will come to me, and wonder, still, what I would do if I knew who he was and saw him today. The man who'd robbed me so early of laughter and innocence. I think I'm capable of putting a gun to the spot between his eyes. I wouldn't hesitate with the trigger. I would watch as his brain burst out the back of his head. Watch as he died. Perhaps if we'd talked, Mom, you would've been able to help. Or, perhaps it would've destroyed you to know.

The sharp smell of camphor filled her nostrils. 'You put grated camphor into the final rinse,' Moena explained. 'For the worms. To keep them away.'

Aqeena wrinkled her nose. She didn't like the smell, and didn't believe the camphor would do anything. How could you prevent rot? The maggots would come from inside: glutting, gorging, irritable as ants on a watermelon pip – the constant scratch at life from the moment of birth.

There was little talking in the room; only what needed to be said. She watched Moena spread a dry sheet over the corpse and remove the damp one underneath. Together, the four of them rolled the body onto its side, towards the centre, and slipped the padded shroud into place. The sheet moved and she caught a glimpse of the face – ivory-coloured, the features softened in death.

Moena took two linen strips, and tied one around the neck, the other around the feet. 'They loosen it when they lay the body down,' she said, 'so the cheek can make contact with the soil.'

Aqeena's heart squeezed in her chest. Contact with the soil! Ashes to ashes, dust to dust. Cold against the damp earth, boxed in under planks. If it rained, the water would fill up the hole and loosen the graveclothes.

She looked down at the mayyit. It was over: 40 years of wiping her nose and holding her hand and always being there at the sewing machine with a smile. There was no more Mom. The lessons had ended. School was out. When the men came in to carry out the mayyit and put it on the bier to walk with it to the mosque, she stayed behind in the room. She didn't go out with the other women to stand on the stoep and in the garden to see her mother off.

We gotta
number there

Richard Cook eased his silver Mercedes into the driveway, the wrought-iron gates closing silently behind him. Seeing a tall African man pacing on the stoep, balling and unballing his fists, gave him a start. His wife, Jennifer, directed his attention to the woman and child sitting under the jacaranda tree, eating sandwiches out of a brown paper bag.

'What a nerve. How did they get in?' he asked.

'Don't lose it, Rick. Just hear what they want.'

Richard switched off the car and got out. The man came down from the stoep, the woman gathering up her things on the lawn, coming towards them, holding the hand of the little girl.

'Good afternoon, boss,' the man started. 'I am Jonas Mbulu and this is – come here, Lucky – my wife, Lucky, and my daughter, Shona.'

'You're trespassing on my property,' Richard Cook said. 'How did you get in?'

Jonas had his cap in his hand, crunching it in a knot. 'We climbed over the gate. I know it's wrong, but we couldn't take the chance that someone else would come to you first.'

'First? First for what?'

'You sacked your gardener, boss. I wanted to apply for the job.

I'm good with my hands. I've looked after gardens and horses and can fix many things.'

Richard looked at his wife. 'How do you know I sacked my gardener?'

'Everyone knows everyone else in Imizamo Yethu, boss. We are five doors from Cyril.'

'Did Cyril tell you why I fired him?'

Jonas hesitated. 'He said he cut your roses without asking, boss, and gave them away. It was for his cousin's funeral.'

'Every single one of them. My whole rose garden. And my dahlias.'

Jonas nodded his head to indicate that he understood. 'He did wrong, boss. His cousin did die, but he did wrong. He could've asked.'

'That's not all. He let one of his friends stay in the house while he went out. The friend took off with the VCR. We need a gardener, but this time we want references.'

Jonas reached into his pocket. It was the moment he'd been waiting for, to be asked for references. 'I have a paper that says where I worked, boss. The telephone number's on it. Lucky has a reference, also. She worked for a madam in Sea Point, but the madam has gone to live in another country. We can both work for you if you'll give us a job. We're honest people, we've been looking for work for a long time. We waited three hours in your garden, boss; give us a chance.'

Richard studied the man with the cap in his hand. Jonas had on clean clothes. He was fit, in his thirties, his wife a slim, young woman standing neatly at his side. It was the little girl, in a hand-me-down navy pleated skirt and white blouse several sizes too big for her, and shoes with laces made out of string, that decided him.

'Let's see the letter.'

Jonas handed it over. Richard read it. He didn't show his surprise. Jonas had worked as a chauffeur and gardener for an American businessman when the company, succumbing to political pressure in 1989, had closed its doors in South Africa and Jonas was let go.

'I would never have left Mr Gordon, boss, but the sanctions cost us all. I haven't been able to find steady work since.'

The Mbulus started work on a trial basis the following day, and soon a routine was established. Jennifer worked as an estate agent in the mornings, and arrived home in the afternoons to find Jonas busy in the garden or in the garage fixing things, Lucky bustling about a spotless house, preparing the meat and vegetables for that night's supper, or pressing Richard's shirts with a precision that greatly pleased him.

One afternoon, Richard came home from work and found Jonas uprooting an old tree. 'I want to talk to you for a minute, Jonas. Can you come inside?'

Jonas washed his face and hands at the tap, and went into the kitchen.

'I've been thinking, Jonas, my stripper's gone back to the Transkei. I can use someone like you at the shop, stripping and refinishing antiques. What do you say, are you interested?'

Jonas's eyes opened slightly at the offer. His face was still wet, and drops of water sat in sparkling crystals in his wiry hair above his forehead and ears. 'A job at the shop, boss?'

'Yes. I can get someone else to do the gardening here, unless you want to do that too. The job at the shop is hard work, but pays double what you get now.'

Jonas glanced at his wife setting down a tea tray in front of Jennifer, who was seated across from her husband at the kitchen table. Lucky's brows rose slightly, but she kept her eyes on the tray.

'Double what I get now, boss?'

'Yes. You would leave with me in the mornings. That means you'd have to be here by seven every day.'

'That's not a problem, boss. I'll be here by six. I would very much like that job. Oh yes. Very much.'

'And the gardening? You have kept it in good shape, Jonas. Once a week should be enough.'

'I'll do that too, boss. We need the money. I could work in the garden a little every night after work, and whole day Sunday if I have to.'

'Sunday's your day off,' Jennifer chimed in.

'That's all right, madam. Lucky and me, we are saving for something. What do I do anyway on a Sunday except sit with my neighbour, Bantu, and his wife and watch television until the battery runs out?'

'Tell them the other thing, Rick,' Jennifer said.

Jonas waited to hear what it was.

Richard took out a cigarette and lit it. 'We've decided to give you the room in the yard. There's a toilet and shower, and I'll build on a small kitchen. It's not big, but you wouldn't have to go back to the squatter camp. You can live here as long as you want.'

'Here, sir?' Lucky asked incredulously. She turned to Jennifer. 'On Madam's premises?'

'Yes,' Jennifer confirmed. 'We don't want anything for it.'

Lucky looked from Jennifer to her husband. 'No one has been this good to us. And the room's not small, madam, it's big. For us it's more than we have. And water right in the kitchen. It's too much.'

'Lucky's right, boss,' Jonas said. 'This is too much good news. A job at the shop, and now you are offering us a place to stay. We don't know how to say thank you. We don't know how, boss, but we can't take it.'

The Cooks looked at each other. 'You can't? Why not?' Richard asked.

Jonas stood upright. 'We've always lived in the Imizamo Yethu village, boss. We don't know any other place. We gotta number there. We feel strong about that number, it's the only thing we have. And the government's offering 80-square-metre sites with a toilet, water and electricity. We're saving for one of those. We want to own our own home. We've never owned a home, boss.'

'That's wonderful, Jonas,' Jennifer said. 'We didn't know you had these plans. How much will a house like that cost?'

'R5000, madam. That's why we are happy for this job. We'll be able to put our names down and have a house by next year. A lot of people are waiting for the free houses the ANC promised. Lucky and me, we don't want anything for free. We want to build our first home in the new South Africa. We want to say Jonas and Lucky did it, and pay for it with our own money.'

Richard inhaled slowly on his cigarette. Jennifer sipped on her tea.

That evening after supper, when the Mbulus had gone home, Jennifer returned to the subject. 'We should help them, Rick. We could help them with the down payment. You can deduct it from Jonas's pay.'

'Let's not jump ahead of ourselves, Jen. Jonas still has to prove himself at the shop.'

'You know he will. Everything he does, he does neatly and with care. Admit it, you couldn't get the rust off that old Mazda. He sanded it down, sealed it, and touched it up. You can get it road-worthied now if you want. We couldn't ask for more honest people. I still can't believe they turned down a room with toilet facilities.'

'How much of a down payment?'

'R1000 or R2000. We can stand surety for the balance. It'll make it easier for them to get a loan. We can also give them Sandra's old bed, it's just taking up space. And the sofa, and some of the chairs.'

Richard waited a month before he spoke to the Mbulus again. He sat them down, and outlined the plan. 'I've already enquired from the RSC the figures involved. I'll take you and Lucky with me to the bank. I'll guarantee the loan. If it's all right with you, I'll deduct R200 a month until you've paid me back. If you're going to borrow R3000 from the bank, I suggest you pay them the same. More, if you can afford it. That way you won't be on their books for too long.'

The Mbulus were stunned by the offer of assistance. Jonas vowed to repay every cent borrowed. Lucky said the Cooks could take half her salary towards the loan.

Richard made an appointment with the manager at his branch, and it was agreed that Jonas would pay R400 a month to the bank. For this they would receive a small house with a veranda, a front door and two windows. There was no insulation, no separate rooms, but the Mbulus could add to it over time.

The months passed. The Mbulus worked hard, and saved. Finally, the big day arrived, and Jennifer drove them in the company van to their new home in the second week in May. It was the first of the government homes. Every neighbour turned out to see the neat little wooden structure with its veranda and potted plant.

Muriel, the lady who sold sheep heads near the bus stop on Fridays, stood with her three sons, watching Lucky and the white madam and Jonas drag the Cooks' old couch off the truck.

'You are lucky, Lucky,' Muriel called to her friend, who was trying not to show how proud she was of her new house.

'I'm not lucky, Muriel,' Lucky said, aware of the people standing around. 'You can also have one.' Muriel lived with her sons in a shack that threatened to lift off over their heads every time the wind blew, and was the most disgruntled person in the neighbourhood.

'We are not so rich', another neighbour chimed in, 'that we have R5000. R5000, isn't it, for one of these? We didn't know you had so much money. Does the madam have a job for us, too?'

'You can go to the bank,' Lucky said. 'And make payments.'

'Who will let us make payments with no jobs?'

'What about your old couch, Lucky? The one with the three legs?' Bertie 'Haircut' called somewhere from the back of the crowd. 'Will you have use for it now that you have such a grand one?'

'You can have it if you want, Bertie,' Jonas said from the top of the truck. 'The house is too small for two couches.'

Muriel wasn't pleased to hear this. 'Lucky, you are letting Jonas give that couch to someone else? I asked you long ago for it. Now you are just giving it to Bertie, who already has that fake velvet sofa that scratches your legs. Has she even given your Shona one free haircut? Look how many times I looked after Shona for you when you went to work.'

Lucky didn't know what to do. 'You never asked for the couch, Muriel. This is the first time I am hearing you want that old thing.'

'Now it's an old thing? Before, you entertained your best friends on it. Perhaps we were not your best friends. Or perhaps you have better things now. Do you have anything else you want to throw out?'

'I have two kitchen chairs,' Lucky said.

'You have new chairs, then?'

'They're not new. I got them from Mrs Cook. This is Mrs Cook. I work for Mrs Cook.'

Muriel turned to Jennifer. 'She is lucky, this Lucky. And she's not called Lucky for nothing. She's lucky to get a man like Jonas. Before, Jonas had a job with a foreigner, and Lucky worked for a good madam in Sea Point. Me and Bertie and some of the others, we're not so lucky. Our husbands left us with children and went off after other women. We have to find things to do where we can look after our children and work.'

Jennifer listened to her complaint, and said she was sorry to hear it. 'You mustn't feel guilty, Lucky,' she said when the three-legged couch and chairs had been given away and the neighbours had moved off. 'You and Jonas have worked hard. You've made your own luck. You deserve this.'

'Yes, madam,' Lucky said uncertainly, a lot of her earlier enthusiasm gone. 'But if we didn't come to work for Madam, we wouldn't have this house. Perhaps we were lucky.'

'You would've done it, anyway. I know you would.'

'Does Madam think so?'

'Of course.'

On a wet afternoon in July, eight weeks later, Richard and Jennifer pulled into the driveway and saw the Mbulus waiting for them on the stoep. It was much like that first day when the Mbulus had come looking for work. Only now there was a heavy curtain of rain sweeping across the lawn, drenching them where they huddled close to the door.

'What're they doing here on a Sunday?' Jennifer asked. 'Something's wrong, I can tell. They're wearing blankets.'

They got out and walked up to the Mbulus. 'What's wrong, Jonas? You look in a state, man,' Richard said. He noticed the blankets, black with soot marks, and smelling strongly of smoke.

Lucky started to sob. Jonas put his arm around her.

Richard turned to the little girl, dressed in a nightie with no shoes on her feet, and a thin blanket over her shoulders. She wasn't a talker on the best of days but looked up at him with big eyes, and said, 'They burn our house ... the other people ...'

Sabah

Sabah parked the car in the strip along Muizenberg beach and opened the door on the passenger side. Tupac jumped off the seat and scampered off. A fractious Alsatian with fierce loyalty, barking at every dark-skinned person coming up the street. She'd called the breeder once, asking if the dog had been trained to attack blacks. 'You should be glad, living in the new Wild West, that he doesn't ask questions first,' he laughed. 'He's a feisty little fucker.'

That's why she'd named him Tupac, after her favourite rapper. Snoop Dogg was one of her favourites also, and Eminem, but Shakur's song to his mama was the best.

'Why you listen to that music, Sabah?' her father had asked her once when she had brought a CD with her and listened to it with him at his house. 'That's not music. You want to listen to music, you put on Charlie Parker.' But he listened to Tupac, and even enjoyed it. He just wanted everyone to love jazz.

Her mother, on the other hand, didn't care if she listened to elevator music as long as she didn't leave South Africa again. 'You can't go back to Canada, my girl. You must promise.'

'I don't have to promise, Mummy. Cape Town's got me.'

Cape Town had changed in her absence. Political violence was down. Murder, robbery and rape were climbing the charts. Homeowners locked their gates, demanding identification before letting service people onto the property. The affluent lived in fortresses with armed response, perimeter lights, infrared beams, panic buttons, and trained Dobermans. There was a new boldness. You couldn't park your vehicle in the city without being bombarded by illegal parking attendants, asking you for money. Fear ruled. The court system sucked. The new President didn't dance. It was life in the windy city.

She liked to be on the beach just after dawn, when the first rays broke through the sky. The shore was smooth then, and untouched, low tide exposing a ripply pattern in the sea sand.

But not that morning. Something had stirred up the ocean, she could hear it. As she walked down to the shore, a thick mist draped itself around her like a diaphanous spectre. She pulled up the collar on her windbreaker. She would never tire of coming here in the mornings, and never walked with people, only with Tupac. They understood one another's silences. She could tell Tupac how she felt, and Tupac didn't have to check a mood calendar to see if he loved her that day.

She reached the water's edge, and stood and looked out at the ocean for a moment. She could feel it more than she could see it, tempestuous and tart – voluptuous waves rolling and crashing about like an old whore.

'Tupac!'

Tupac materialised out of the haze, and found his place next to her. They started their walk. It was dangerous to walk woman-alone down to Strandfontein, Jeremy always said. But she wasn't afraid. She never allowed herself to think about it. The beach was hers, with the seagulls and the seaweed and the wind slapping into her loose pants. Walking along the shore was where she figured out beginnings, middles and endings. Since her return six years ago, she'd had one beginning and one ending. And then another beginning.

Her friend Billie had not held out much hope for her. 'You'll never be able to live there for good, Sabah. You won't have the patience for a fledgling democracy. I give it six months, then you're back. Look at the luxuries we have here. Free medical aid. The best transportation system in the world. You can sleep with your door open at night.'

'But can you smell the sea, Billie?'

'There's more to life than the sea. When you were living there, were you on the beach every day? Canada's been good for you.'

'You're going to miss me, Billie. I know. But you know where I'll be. Why don't you come and live there for a few years?'

Billie had been right about a lot of things, especially about Canada. Had she never left South Africa in 1968, she would've been a different person today. Canada had healed her, then given her back. How would she ever forget? Canada had been her adoptive mother, but mothers also had to let go. And she had found her feet. Her life had taken on a new rhythm. She walked, she wrote, she saw Jeremy two nights a week. Two nights was ample. More than that would force her to look ahead. She didn't want to. She knew she could never have him for good. She wasn't sad. She'd lived long enough to know that you could love one man as well as another. It was all a matter of cleaning the palette between them. When she cut it with Shafiq, she stopped playing Pink Floyd. Listening to it, even now, could still make her feel the touch of his hand as he brushed her hair out of her neck. But she'd changed to Miles Davis. In time she got used to a different laugh, a different beat, longer legs next to hers. Her friendship with Jeremy was in the right place. Jeremy talked of a summer house in Betty's Bay. He didn't question the future. Not yet. But, one day, she knew, one of them would, and then it would end. That day, she hoped she still felt the same way. She couldn't change the music forever.

'I'm wild about you, luv, but we want different things.'

'What do I want?'

'You want forever.'

'Don't be so fucking arrogant.'

She thought of dinner the previous night at Café Matisse with Adam. She and Adam had been friends since high school. At twenty, she went off to Canada. Adam went on to defend criminals. His children were adults now, he said, he didn't have to stay, but couldn't leave his wife who'd been loyal to him through the years. Sabah didn't want him to leave his wife for her. She wanted only friendship. But even the friendship wasn't without problems. Emotional closeness with another woman was threatening – what woman would like it? If anyone had seen them walking in Kalk Bay at midnight, they wouldn't have believed they were just friends. But she'd never touched him, never wanted to. And Adam was too straight to cheat.

'Forget about Jeremy,' he said. 'Look in my eyes and fall in love with me.'

'I'm not second-wife material, my angel.'

'You don't even have to move to Oranjezicht. You can move straight to Camps Bay. I'll sweeten the package.'

'Who gets the extra day?'

'You do.'

They'd laughed, then returned to talking about Jeremy.

'It's too bad he's so spooked. He's got what you want. He might even be good for you.'

'Last week you said he wasn't.'

'I know, but who am I to give advice? When I leave here, I go home to my wife. You're alone.'

Alone was a big word. How many friends she had who suffered from it. Teresa. Billie. She too at one time, before she'd learned to accept it and make it her friend. Billie had cried after her break-up with Marge. 'She's a bitch, Sabah. All this time I'm thinking she's faithful to me, and she's carrying on with that trollop down at the Post Office.'

Sabah smiled as she remembered that she herself hadn't known at the time Billie came with her to South Africa for a holiday, that Billie was gay. By the time she discovered it, Billie was in love with her. She had had to put Billie straight – 'I like boys, Billie. No girl's going to be pulling down my panties.' The friendship was strengthened, and soon after, Billie's heart was set on a new secretary who had joined the firm.

Sabah thought of her friend Jehaan in Athlone. Jehaan was wife number one and didn't at all mind the secretary her husband had married.

'To tell you the truth, Sabah, at least I know where he is, and I don't have to sleep with him every night. You get tired of all that slobber and sex. She's making it easier for me.'

Sabah admired her generosity. Jehaan could've left him and taken him for half of everything, but didn't. Her shock at discovering that she'd been betrayed made her lose the twenty pounds she'd tried ten years to shed, her new figure giving her confidence and a whole new attitude. She had the house, the BMW, and the housekeeping allowance, but now also had the freedom to do what she wanted four times a week.

'She can have the extra day. I'm better off for it. I don't have to cook for him. And when we get together now, he's so glad to see me, we do things he never would've done before. There's that guilt, you know, being able to have two women with God's consent. But God didn't consent to lust, and they know it. They don't talk about the reasons. They just tell you they're allowed. But it's worked out for me. After twenty years with the same man, you get bored also. Do they think we don't look at other men? If I'm you, I would marry Adam. You'll have a man when you need one, and still have your freedom. It's a heck of a deal.'

But she couldn't do it – not to another woman, and not to herself. And she didn't feel that way about Adam. They had a history, but life had intersected. He represented the past; Jeremy, what she'd gotten used to. One was a spiritual guide, the other wanted unrestricted conjugal rights. What she needed was a man from her own culture. But what was her culture and how did she fit into it?

'I have the same feelings as you, but we're different people.'

'You mean I'm a Muslim and you're a Jew.'

'Something like that. We don't have to let it affect anything.' But she knew in the end it would. It would be the reason to separate.

A low growl from Tupac made her look up. They were at an isolated spot on the beach, the road running alongside it concealed by high dunes on their left. She tried to see what had disturbed the Alsatian, but couldn't see anything.

Then she saw them rise out of the mist, three youths coming over the dunes. She knew instinctively that it was danger. They weren't there for the aesthetics. It was in the stride, the way they drifted slowly towards her. It was what all the warnings had been about.

Her heart knocked under her shirt. There were no houses in the vicinity, no joggers. She was alone. She had rejected the advice, except Jeremy's, to get a gun. She hadn't told her mother, not even Jeremy, but had bought one and taken lessons at the firing range and had once worn it clipped to her belt when she drove to Port Elizabeth for a friend's wedding. What had made her wear it that day?

'Guns are dangerous, Sabah. People get killed with their own weapons. If you're ever faced with danger, don't think. Shoot!

You won't get a second chance.'

But it was easy to receive advice in the safety of your living room. Without turning her head she watched them approach. Coloured boys. Young. Cocky. They were less than twenty feet away, coming quickly. She could see the grin of the one taking the lead.

She slipped her hand under her sweatshirt and felt the cold smoothness of the snub-nosed gun. She was frighteningly calm. Not out of courage; out of fear. Her eyes never left the one in front. He'd taken out a knife, walking faster than the others.

Then, everything happened all at once, and they ran towards her. From nowhere the gun appeared in her hand. The shot crackled over their heads and they jumped back in fright. Tupac leapt, and brought down the leader.

'Who wants to fuck me!' she snarled.

The leader rolled about screaming at her feet, trying frantically to protect his face from the dog.

'Who wants to fuck me!' The gun was pointed at the other two, going from one face to the other. 'I can do it! Don't fuck with me! I can do it!'

The other two turned on their heels, and bolted. Tupac charged after them. The leader struggled to his feet, and ran off. In seconds they were swallowed up by the fog.

Sabah remained standing with the gun in her hand. Her heart thumped a death march in her ears. She stood very still. The knife, at her feet, glinted faintly in the sand.

'Tupac!'

The mist was thick on all sides, she couldn't see. The drama had unfolded suddenly and quickly, without witnesses.

The Alsatian returned and she continued on to Strandfontein. Tomorrow she would think. Now she just had to put one foot in front of the other and keep walking.